They had said goodbye W9-BAM-537 **and she really hadn't expected to see him again.**

And she knew her brother had been trying to get them together again or he would never have sent a present for the baby and asked Noah to place it in Ethan's hands.

"I'll call you before I come out," Noah added, looking at her.

"Please do call. My schedule varies."

"You look great, Camilla," he said, and his voice suddenly had a rasp that made her pulse jump.

"Thank you. So do you," she whispered.

"I don't know why the hell you fell in love with me when you knew from day one that my life is on the ranch," he said. His eyes blazed with a mix of anger and desire and a muscle worked in his jaw.

Her temper flared, too, and she leaned closer to him, breathing deeply and locking her gaze on his mouth. "Oh, I think you know full well why I fell in love with you."

* * *

The Rancher's Heir is part of
Harlequin Desire's #1 bestselling series,
Billionaires and Babies: Powerful men...wrapped
around their babies' little fingers.

Dear Reader,

An honorable man keeps his promises. This series is about three friends making promises to their dying US Army Ranger buddy, with each vow involving a life-changing event.

The second former US Army Ranger to keep his promise is Noah Grant, who returns home to Dallas, Texas, and to the West Texas ranch he loves, bearing gifts for the woman he's never forgotten.

Before leaving for the army, Noah's affair with Camilla Warner ended because his life choices reminded her of painful events in her past. He also is a cowboy at heart in spite of his fortune, and she is a city person who loves opera, art and city life. While Noah was in the military, Camilla married. Two months later she was divorced and pregnant. Now, over a year later, Noah is back.

This story involves family, close friends and a passionate love between two people with different lifestyles separating them, but who are still irresistibly drawn to each other.

Thank you for your interest in this book, and best wishes. Please find me at saraorwig.com or on Facebook as Sara Orwig, Romance Writer.

Sara Orwig

SARA ORWIG

THE RANCHER'S HEIR

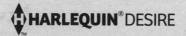

Recycling programs
for this product may
not exist in your area.

ISBN-13: 978-1-335-97161-6

The Rancher's Heir

Printed in U.S.A.

HARLEQUIN
www.Harlequin.com

An explosion rocked the ground not twenty feet away, sending up a plume of light. Mike turned to punch Noah's shoulder. As Noah Grant lowered his weapon, Mike told him, "Trade places. Keep pressure on his wounds. He wants to talk to you."

Without hesitation, Noah took Mike Moretti's place, holding Thane's own jacket and Mike's jacket over Thane's wounds, trying to apply pressure to the two most serious ones, hoping his captain and friend could hang on until help arrived.

Thane gripped his arm and Noah leaned closer to hear him over the explosives. With shallow breathing and a hoarse whisper, Thane spoke through obvious pain. "Noah, promise me you'll take two gifts home for me." Coughs racked his body and he grimaced. "Promise me."

"I promise," Noah said without thinking as he concentrated on trying to keep pressure on the wounds.

"Two keys in pocket," Thane said in a raspy, weakened voice, placing his hand on a pocket. "Keys alike. Other one for Jake. Mike has one."

"Don't talk. Save your strength." Trying to keep pressure on the wounds, Noah slipped his hand into the pocket, leaning down closer to Thane. "I have the keys."

Thane's eyelids fluttered and he looked at Noah. "…in box…two packages go to Camilla and Ethan." He closed his eyes and stopped talking. Noah leaned closer.

"Thane. Thane. Hang in there. Chopper's coming. Thane!"

Prologue

During the night under a starless sky, they had driven their Humvee into an ambush, and now they were barely holding on, pinned down in a firefight with nothing but a crumbling rock wall between them and the enemy. Noah Grant had only cuts and bruises. His two close friends, Mike Moretti and Jake Ralston, also had non-life-threatening injuries. The other member on this US Army Rangers mission, Captain Thane Warner, was hurt badly with wounds to his chest and head, an injured leg and deep gashes all over his body from flying shrapnel.

Mike had applied pressure to two serious wounds, trying to save their captain and friend until help arrived. Their last communication had been cut off, but before it was, Noah heard a chopper was on the way.

Sara Orwig, from Oklahoma, loves family, friends, dogs, books, long walks, sunny beaches and palm trees. She is married to and in love with the guy she met in college. They have three children and six grandchildren. Sara's 100th published novel was a July 2016 release. With a master's degree in English, she has written historical romance, mainstream fiction and contemporary romance. Sara welcomes readers on Facebook or at saraorwig.com.

Books by Sara Orwig

Harlequin Desire

Callahan's Clan

Expecting the Rancher's Child
The Rancher's Baby Bargain
The Rancher's Cinderella Bride
The Texan's Baby Proposal

Texas Promises

Expecting a Lone Star Heir
The Rancher's Heir

Visit her Author Profile page at Harlequin.com, or saraorwig.com, for more titles.

Thane's eyes fluttered and he grasped Noah's wrist with surprising strength. "Promise…you'll give Camilla…gift yourself."

"I promise I'll put her gift in her hands," he said, not wanting to think about actually doing the deed.

"Other present—promise me…you…give to my nephew…have to…give to him, no one else…want him to see a soldier. Don't give to Camilla… Promise me even though—"

"I promise to put the present in your nephew's hands myself."

Thane's eyes fluttered open and for an instant Noah felt a shock as Thane looked intently at him.

"I promise to place it in the baby's hands," Noah repeated emphatically, startled by the piercing look from Thane.

The last statement seemed to pacify him as he nodded and closed his eyes. "Get Jake."

Noah looked around, spotted Jake and shouted at him. He didn't dare let go of the blood-soaked jackets he held against Thane's wounds.

"Jake," he shouted again and jerked his head when Jake looked around.

Noah turned back to tell Thane that Jake was coming. Anxiety filled him as he saw Thane's eyes were closed, his head turned away. Noah felt for a pulse and was surprised to find one. "Thane," he shouted, trying to keep the man awake until medics arrived. "Thane, stay with me."

Jake slipped down beside Noah just as another explosion ripped the ground in front of them. "Thane wants you to have this key," Noah said, handing a small key to his friend. "He'll tell you what he wants you to do. Hold these against his wounds. Where the hell is the chopper?"

"I don't know, but last I heard it's coming."

"It better get here soon. He's lost too much blood." He leaned close to Thane's ear.

"Thane, here's Jake," Noah shouted and moved away as Jake took over keeping pressure on Thane's wounds.

"Hang on, Thane. Help is coming," Jake shouted, leaning close to Thane as the man stared blankly at him.

Noah moved away, pausing when he heard another sound besides the bursts of gunfire and the explosion of a grenade. Were they going to get some help? He opened his hand that was smeared with Thane's dried blood. A brass key lay in his palm and Noah drew a deep breath. He didn't want to go home and give Camilla a gift from Thane. When they broke up, he didn't expect to ever be with her again and it still hurt to think about her.

He didn't want to see her, talk to her or do anything to stir up old feelings. It had hurt to walk away but he had and now he had to go back to her. He wondered whether he would ever reach a point where he would stop thinking about her.

One

Noah

Six months later, in July, Noah was no longer a Ranger in the US Army. He'd been honorably discharged, armed now with a list of things he needed to do before he settled back into civilian life and took over his ranch again. He'd systematically run through the list until, after tonight, there was only one thing left to do—take Thane's packages to Camilla and her baby. He didn't want to see either of them, but he would keep his promise to Thane. He stood holding two packages. He guessed the one for her baby was a book—that was what it felt like. Both packages were wrapped in what looked like the brown paper of grocery sacks at home. Used paper with wrinkles smoothed out. The other package for Camilla was a box. It wasn't deep, but it was bigger than the book. Each one was tied with brown twine. Neither box felt heavy. A simple delivery. Just hand them to her and get the hell out of her life again. Just the thought of seeing her was stirring up too many unwanted memories.

The first weekend back he'd gone home to see his parents in Dallas. He'd hugged his mother while Betsy Grant had wiped away tears as she smiled at him.

"Mom, don't cry," he'd said.

"I'm just so happy you're home."

"I'm happy to be home and I'll never understand crying for happiness."

Smiling, she'd wiped her eyes and patted his cheek. "Someday you will. Someday you'll have tears of joy and relief in your eyes."

"Don't wish that on me," he'd said, laughing. As he'd hugged her, he'd realized she felt a lot more frail than she had when he had hugged her goodbye before he'd left for Afghanistan.

His dad's handshake had been firm, his smile as warm as ever, but Cal Grant's skin had looked pale.

Tonight he returned to the family Tudor mansion in Dallas and walked in to see his siblings. Noah stepped to Hallie to hug her lightly. His sister-in-law was still a beautiful woman, tall, blonde and brown-eyed.

"We're glad you're home," she said, smiling at him.

He turned to his middle brother and gazed into blue eyes slightly lighter than his own. The two looked alike, except Ben had wavy black hair, not thick black curls like Noah. Noah wrapped his arms around Ben, Hallie's husband, and hugged him. "I'm glad to see you," he said, meaning it.

"I'm glad you're here, bro. Eli was sorry he couldn't get here tonight. He couldn't get out of a dinner where he's a speaker."

"I'll see him soon."

"Come sit and let everyone talk to you," his mother said as they all walked into the big familiar living room with comfortable sofas and chairs. "You can't imagine how glad we all are that you're home."

He sat and talked to his family and once again he was struck by how much his parents had aged in the years he'd been in the military. He heard the front door open, and then his sister, Stefanie, appeared, screeching when she saw Noah. She ran across the room, her black hair flying, to throw her arms around his neck. Laughing, he hugged her and she stepped back, smiling at him.

"I'm so glad you're home."

He looked into her deep blue eyes, so like his own, and smiled. "I'm glad to be home."

She turned to greet the rest of the family, crossing the room to kiss their dad's cheek, going to brush her mother's cheek with a kiss. "This is a celebration," she said.

Noah laughed. Some things never changed, and his little sister stirring up the whole family with her grand entrance was one of those things.

And some things did change, he thought. Like his parents.

As they all sat and talked, he realized how good it was to be home. Nothing was more important than family. This was what he'd wanted at some point in his life. The moment that thought came, so did memories of Camilla and, with them, an unwanted pang that shocked him. After all this time, how could he still miss her? They had broken up three years ago and he didn't want to still miss her. He didn't want to picture her when he thought of having his own family. But he did. She was his wife and the mother of his children in all such fantasies.

But it had to stop. Now.

Banishing those tormenting images, he turned to his father and tried to pay attention to what the man was saying. It wasn't until ten that night, when his folks said good-night and retired for the evening, that he was alone with Ben and Hallie and Stefanie.

"C'mon, Stefanie. Come with me. I'm going to find a book to take home," Hallie said, dragging his sister to the library down the hall.

Noah looked at Ben. "I know the folks usually tell us good-night and leave, but Hallie has left for a reason besides getting a book to read."

"Yeah. Let's go into the study," Ben said, and Noah realized it was something serious. He followed his brother.

Ben switched on the lights and Noah glanced

around the familiar room that served as his dad's home office. Then his attention shifted to Ben.

"What's up? I have the feeling there's something you've been waiting to tell me."

"There is. I told Mom I would tell you and you can talk to them about it tomorrow, but she can't talk without crying."

"Oh, damn," Noah said, sinking into a leather chair. Instantly he remembered his dad's pallor and quiet manner. "It's Dad, isn't it?"

"You noticed. I figured you would. He—he has heart problems. Since you've been gone, he's had a heart attack and he's had bypass surgery."

Noah felt as if he had been punched in the chest. He hurt and he looked down, remembering his dad in earlier years. "Dammit."

Ben took a seat beside him. "Dad isn't strong any longer, but he walks on a treadmill several times nearly every day."

Noah looked away, remembering moments as a kid when he'd had fun with his dad, playing ball, swimming.

"That's a hell of a thing to come home to," he told Ben. "How's Stefanie handling it?"

"She's hovering over him, which seems to make them both happy. Mom, too. Between work and her social life, Stefanie keeps busy, so she's okay. She's running the north Dallas Grant Realty office and she's very good at it." He shook his head as if amazed at how well she handled the family's real-estate business. "I thought she was too much a social butterfly to be a sharp businesswoman, but I was wrong. Last spring, she spent a month in our south Texas home and had it all done over. And I think she has plans for the Colorado home this fall. I don't know where she gets the energy. Even with all that on her plate, she moves in social circles and supports several chari-ties. I've got about three I devote time, effort and money to, while Eli has about five. You know how Dad taught us all we need to give back to the com-munity, so here we are, doing what he expected."

"I'm sure he's proud of you all."

Ben looked at him squarely. "We're all proud of you serving in the Army in the Rangers."

Noah shrugged. "Our dad served. Our grandfather. Our great-grandfather. It's a family tradition. But one from this generation is enough. Don't you go sign up."

Ben held up his hands, palms out. "No danger of that. I have my hands full here." He ran a hand through his hair. "When Dad had to step down, I took over the main real-estate office. You know, it might be a good thing if you come in about once or twice a month just so you know what's going on and you're able to take over if I'm away."

"Okay, but I'm sure you have some vice presidents who can step in."

"Oh, yes. I just want you to know about the busi-ness since Dad is out."

"And in turn you'll come out to the ranch and spend a couple of days per month."

"Noah, ranching is your deal and maybe Eli's occasionally. I would be lousy—"

Noah laughed and waved his hand. "Don't worry. I'm kidding. You barely know a horse's head from its rear, so I don't think you'd be of much help anyway."

Ben sat back, looking relieved. "Don't scare me like that." Then he sobered. "Back to Dad. I told him I'd tell you about his heart. He said he has a doctor's appointment tomorrow and they're running some tests. He said to give him a couple of days and then come by. I think those doctor appointments wear him out. So much that he doesn't even venture into the office any longer." Ben leaned forward. "Don't panic, Noah, but I'd really like you on the board."

"The ranch is my life. I'll be on the board, but I won't take an office job." He got up and paced the den. "You know, when you leave home, you think you're coming back to the same life, but you never do," he said. "Well, hell, this one hurts and it's just going to hurt more as the days go by." He stared into space a moment, lost again in memories of his dad. He turned to Ben. "Thanks for telling me."

"Yeah. I hated to have to tell you."

"I'm glad I didn't know it over there. Losing Thane was hell enough. We've been friends since we were schoolkids. His wounds were too bad and they couldn't save him. How're things with you?"

Ben shrugged. "Business is good. On the home front there have been some tense moments—" He paused to look at Noah. "Hallie and I have tried since we first married to have a baby. Especially since Dad's heart problems. We wanted him to know his first grand-child." Ben shook his head and glanced at the closed door. "The docs say we're both okay, to just relax, that pregnancy will happen. It would give Mom and Dad so much pleasure." He paused a moment as Noah resumed his seat, then met his brother's eyes. "I hate to ask, but...have you seen Camilla?"

At the mere mention of her name, his insides knot-ted. "No, but I will. Thane asked me to take gifts to her and to her baby."

"She was only married two, three months at most. Then the guy was gone. He was there long enough that she has a baby. He left town before their divorce and I've heard he doesn't have any interest in the kid."

"Doesn't matter. It's over between us," Noah said, his stomach tightening even more. "I'm too much the alpha male for her, which is the pot calling the kettle black, to quote the old saying. And she loves Dallas and won't even visit my ranch."

"Sorry. You two seemed close."

They had been once. They'd dated for a year before he joined the Army. "Not any longer." Noah stood. "I better go and let you get home."

They walked back to rejoin the others. He glanced at Stefanie. "If I know you, you're just getting ready to start your evening. You're probably meeting friends."

Smiling, she wrinkled her nose at him. "You might be right. You can even join us."

"Thanks, but not tonight." He turned to his brother. "I'll call and see Dad when it's convenient for him."

Ben nodded, then reached out to hug his brother.

"Damn, I'm glad you're home," he said.

"Let me know if you need me. I have something I need to do in Dallas before I go to the ranch and I'll spend a bit longer in Dallas to be with Dad more."

"That will be good. I'm sorry about you and Camilla."

It still hurt too much to talk about her. "Thanks. So am I, but I'm not giving up ranching. I sure as hell can't change my personality."

He said good-night to Stefanie and Hallie. "See you both soon," Noah said as he made his way to the door.

Stefanie asked him to wait, walking outside with him.

"How is it with Camilla?" she asked as they headed toward her car. "Have you seen her baby?"

"It's finished with Camilla, and no, I haven't seen her baby," he said.

"Sorry, Noah, if you're unhappy about it. Come out with me Friday night and have some fun."

He laughed and squeezed her shoulder. "You'd take the old man out with you? Thanks, but I'll pass this time."

"You're not that much older than my crowd and you're not as old as some of them." She smiled at him and touched his arm. "Think about it. Also, I'm a co-chairman for the Heart Ball—"

He stopped her with a grin. "I'll take a table and however many tickets that means."

"Ahhh, thank you! It's still three months away but it's never too soon to sell tickets." She opened her red sports car and turned back to him. This time he noticed her expression had sobered. "Ben told you about Dad, didn't he?"

"Yeah, he did. I'll go by and talk to Dad soon. He has a doctor's appointment tomorrow."

"It breaks my heart, but I don't want to be sad around them. He seems to be doing okay, but I'm sure you see a difference."

"Of course I do." He reached out to her. "If you want a shoulder to cry on, I've got one."

She gazed up at him. "There will be times I'll need it. You're a wonderful big brother."

He smiled and pulled her to him in a hug. When he released her, he held open her car door, then closed it when she was in. "See you soon," he said as he turned for his car. As he opened his car door, he glanced back to see her backing out of her parking place. He left, driving to the condo he maintained in Dallas while he thought about his dad, and then his thoughts shifted to Camilla. He would see her—after all this time. His pulse beat faster when he thought about her while at the same time memories of the past clutched at his heart. He had put this meeting off long enough. Even though it might very well open old wounds, the time had come to see her and fulfill his promise.

Stefanie

Stefanie drove to her condo in downtown Dallas. She ran a family office in a suburban area, but she liked the town condo. When she was inside, she walked to the window to look out at the city without really seeing it. Her thoughts were lost on her oldest brother. She was thankful he was home. Noah had a steadying influence on everyone in the family.

She could hear the gruffness in his voice when she had asked about Camilla, and her anger flashed. She'd liked Camilla—until she'd hurt Noah. She'd hurt him before he ever left for overseas and that had worried Stefanie. She'd feared he wouldn't have his mind on his job as much if he was worried about Camilla—something that could be fatal in hostile territory.

She thought about Camilla, who was pursuing an art career. Stefanie had always wondered if she had married to spite Noah because her husband was gone in a couple of months. Camilla probably hadn't planned on a pregnancy. The guy hadn't even wanted his baby.

Stefanie thought about Noah, looking preoccupied tonight, learning about their dad and coming home to unhappiness with Camilla. Noah needed to meet someone, someone who was fun to be with, someone who would get him over his breakup.

Stefanie knew some really gorgeous women who would be perfect for Noah. She knew two women in particular who came to mind right away. Better still, one of them was going to be in Vivian Warner's wedding party when Thane's widow remarried next week. She could call Vivian. Noah needed someone who would make him happy.

And Stefanie needed to think of a way to get Camilla away from Dallas and out of her brother's life.

If Camilla was away from Dallas, maybe Noah would be more interested in going out and meeting new friends.

Camilla

In her large art studio at her Dallas home, Camilla stepped back to look at the canvas on an easel. She had a commissioned family portrait of two children she was painting from a picture she had taken with her iPad. She usually got up early to paint while Ethan slept. She would hear him on the monitor when he stirred.

It was quiet, peaceful in her studio, and on breaks from painting, she could watch the sunrise over her backyard.

Light spilled into the room and over easels holding watercolor paintings, charcoal drawings and portraits. One wall held a massive landscape painting. There were shelves filled with art bottles of acrylic paints and tubes of oils. Two sinks were near a worktable. Sunshine splashed through the floor-to-ceiling glass wall that gave a broad view of her gardens. Stacks of drawings and prints were in bins along a wall. She had a patio door open to let fresh air in and a slight paint smell out. She had a studio in her condo, another studio in an office in downtown Dallas, but this was her favorite place to paint. She also had an art gallery in Dallas.

As she cleaned her brushes, she glanced over at a black-and-white pencil sketch propped on top of a cabinet holding her paints. The sketch was Noah, one she had done from a picture after they started dating. She still liked it. All in shades of black and gray on a white background, she had made his eyes a vivid blue, trying to reproduce the color of them. He had a faint smile and his black hair was its usual unruly tangle. That mass of tangled curls was gone when she last saw him with his military cut.

She stared at his picture a moment, dreading seeing him again while at the same time missing him, wondering what the future held. Guilt plagued her and memories taunted her, memories of his kisses, moments in his arms.

With a shake of her head, she continued to put away brushes and pencils. In the cabinet were scrapbooks with printouts of pictures and artwork she had done.

She had attended a musical at the Music Hall last night, and during the performance, her mind had wandered to Noah. He was out of the military now.

On the wall behind a massive wooden desk was a wall calendar with the art jobs she had pending and due dates. She had appointments written in, important events she would attend, including her widowed sister-in-law's upcoming wedding. Noah would be there and their paths would cross.

She thought over what she'd heard: Noah Grant was home. She couldn't get him out of her thoughts. She couldn't understand her reaction to hearing the news. She hadn't seen him for two years, not since he'd been home on furlough. Even back then he was exactly what she disliked in a man—a take-charge male—yet when she heard he was back, her heart had raced and longing shook her. For just an instant, she forgot their fights and arguments and remembered only the good moments. Noah making her laugh, Noah holding her, kissing her. Noah taking her to bed, where she'd run her hands over his smooth back. Noah—

Stop it.

She had to listen to that sane inner voice telling her to rein in those errant memories. Yes, they'd had moments of ecstasy, of bliss, but those times were over.

So why did the mere anticipation of seeing him make her heart flutter? Why did she have such an intense reaction to him?

Their last time together had ended in a bitter breakup and she had been the one who'd enacted it. She told him they had no future. She had a father who made all the decisions and ran their house with an iron fist. All her life her mother had given in to her dad. Too far back to remember exactly when, Camilla had vowed she would never live a life where she had to constantly give in to someone else about everything. She had to make some of her own decisions beyond what she would wear and whom she'd invite to the next party.

Her brother, as much as she had loved Thane, had been another take-charge man. But she wouldn't allow herself to choose a man like that for a husband.

At least her dad led a quiet life. Noah, on the other hand, liked challenges.

Noah and she were such opposites that she couldn't understand the attraction she felt. She was going to Shakespeare in the Park tonight. Noah would never go with her to Shakespeare, the opera or the ballet. He seldom went to art galleries with her. She loved city life, operas, chamber music, her art. Noah was a billionaire rancher, but a cowboy at heart. He loved his ranch, boot-scootin' honky-tonks, country music, competing in rodeos, flying his planes. He was exuberant, filled with life, and he'd take charge wherever he was. She didn't want to tie her life to a cowboy who was 100 percent determined to do things his way.

So why did she almost melt when she looked into his vivid blue eyes? Why did his kisses set her on fire? He could make her forget the world, forget what she liked and didn't like. So easily he could make her want to be in his arms. And that was what he had done the last time she had seen him when he had come home to Texas on a furlough.

They had started out fighting and arguing and

ended up in bed in each other's arms. He had charmed her as he usually did.

For all their differences and her wanting to avoid getting entangled with a wild, take-charge rancher who liked challenges, she had been charmed, dazzled and unable to resist the mutual attraction, and she had spent the weekend in his bed. Now she was going to face the consequences.

When Noah had been home on furlough, he had been more appealing than ever. He had filled out with broad, muscled shoulders, a hard body in prime shape with a narrow waist, endurance that made him fabulous in bed. Just thinking about seeing him again made her pulse race and her insides get tingly.

She didn't know how she would deal with him. No matter how much she planned to stand firm, to resist him, she feared that all he had to do was wrap his arm around her and kiss her and her resistance would disappear into thin air.

On the other hand, he could be stubborn, determined and unyielding. Which made her wonder how forgiving he could be. She couldn't answer that, because there hadn't ever been an occasion between them for her to gauge his ability to forgive.

Thinking of seeing Noah made her shiver.

She heard the monitor and left to get her fifteen-month-old son.

He had gone back to sleep and she stood beside his crib, love filling her for her baby. Ethan lay curled on his side. His long black lashes cast dark shadows on his rosy cheeks.

Camilla ran her fingers lightly over her precious sleeping baby. His mop of curly black hair reminded her of his dad. He held a frazzled-looking teddy bear in his arms—the toy he held like a security blanket whenever he'd get sleepy. The bear's stitched black nose was smashed from Ethan rubbing noses with it.

She touched Ethan's curls again. Guilt was a heavy shroud that had fallen over her. This was Noah's baby and he had no idea that Ethan was his son.

Two

Camilla

All during her pregnancy, everyone assumed she was carrying her ex-husband Aiden's child. When she realized they did, she let everyone go right on believing that. By the second month after they married, Aiden and she were divorced. When the baby was born, it was easy to keep up the deception. She had been divorced and Aiden had left town six months before Ethan was born, so no one questioned her naming her baby Warner, her family name. Aiden had been a rebound marriage, a fling, a mistake, and she never wanted to keep his name and he had no interest in her baby.

Little Ethan, like Aiden and Noah, had black hair, so no one suspected anything.

Though she'd already broken up with Noah when she started dating Aiden, she'd been pregnant. Noah had been back in Afghanistan, his furlough over. As well as their relationship.

She'd known Aiden since college and she married him on the rebound. She had thought he would be a dad for her baby, but she knew the second week of the marriage she had made a mistake and she felt he wasn't happy, either.

They really weren't compatible. By the second month he'd wanted a divorce and so had she.

People still didn't realize this was Noah's baby. While guilt plagued her because Noah had a right to know the truth, she knew he would want to take charge of the situation. He would want control over her baby. Maybe her own life in some ways would be out of her hands.

At some point she had to let him know about Ethan, but she dreaded it more than anything in her life. She was not going to let him know yet. Ethan was the joy of her life now. She didn't want to lose him. Nor was she ready to share him. Noah was a rancher, but she loved city life and wanted her son in Dallas.

Though she'd spent time on her grandfather's ranch, she wasn't fond of them. Being on a ranch made her think of Winston, her little brother who had fallen through the ice at their grandfather's ranch when Winston was four. Thane had pulled him out of the icy pond. Later Winston had developed pneumonia and died. It always saddened her to think of that time.

The entire year they'd dated, Noah had never declared his love, but he'd made it clear that if he ever wanted to marry, his wife would have to live on his ranch.

Yes, suffice it to say, she and Noah had hugely different lifestyles. Noah wasn't going to change and she didn't want to change, either.

She brushed her fingers so lightly over Ethan's soft curls, feeling them tickle the palm of her hand. Wanting to lean down and kiss him, she resisted because she was afraid she would wake him. The minute Noah knew about their son, she was certain he would want to take charge of Ethan's life and maybe hers, too. She would see Noah when Mike Moretti and Thane's widow, Vivian, married. Their wedding was coming up this next weekend, and both she and Noah would be in it. Ethan was too little to go to this wedding, so she didn't have to worry about having Noah and Ethan in the same place.

Aside from Mike and Vivian, she moved in a circle of friends now who did not know Noah, so she hoped she'd be able to drag out the deception a little longer.

Over the last almost two years there'd been times she'd considered telling Noah about his son, but she'd always backed off. Now, as she looked at her baby and fought the urge to hold him in her arms, she knew despite her guilty conscience, she had to continue to keep Noah away from him. It was too terrifying to tell him the truth.

Noah

Tuesday afternoon, Noah sat across from Mike as they ate burgers together on the patio of a popular lunch place in Dallas. "I'm glad about you and Thane's widow," Noah told his friend. "I guess it was good you told Thane you'd go to work for him when you got out of the military. I think it gave him peace of mind to hire you and know if something happened to him, you'd go home to run the ranch. He may have hoped all along that you would marry Vivian."

"I'm sure he was taking care of Vivian and taking care of his beloved ranch. He had everything all lined up if anything happened to him." Mike put down his burger and wiped his mouth on a napkin. "Now you have an errand for him."

"Right," Noah said, looking into his friend's alert brown eyes. Mike's black hair had a slight wave and was longer than when he was in the service, but still cut short. "I had to promise Thane I would put his package into Camilla's hands myself. The baby, too. Her baby isn't going to know or care what's going on and probably won't even know he has a present."

Mike laughed. "Thane probably hoped you'd get back with his sister."

"That won't happen. She told me a definite goodbye and she married after I left. She divorced him a few months into the marriage and now has his baby. Camilla and I are history. I'm too much the alpha male for her."

"We're all alpha males, and her brother definitely was, too."

"She has said the same thing about her brother." Noah shrugged. "I can't change something as basic as that. It's who I am. I don't know how we got together in the first place. We're opposites. She likes opera, art galleries and big cities. I like my country-western music, rodeos and the ranch. In short, we were never meant to be. It's over."

"Sorry. Life can get complicated. Thane probably wanted you to get back together so that her child would have a good dad around."

"She's from a very wealthy family. In addition, she does well with her art, some pieces bringing big bucks before I left for the service. She does watercolor landscapes, murals, also portraits and has done some portraits for celebs for impressive amounts of money, so she doesn't need one bit of financial help. Also, she has two more brothers, Mason and Logan. As far as I know, they'll be around some for her baby. When I left for the service Mason had a financial consulting firm in Austin and Logan is head of his Dallas oil company. Maybe being in a war made Thane sentimental. I don't know. All I have to do is take the present to her and give the baby his present and say goodbye."

Mike paused as he went to take another bite of

his burger, and his eyes met Noah's. "Sorry, buddy. She'll be in our wedding because she's family and a friend of Vivian's."

"It won't matter. While it's over between us, we can be civil to each other. I'll see her at your wedding and then it's goodbye and we probably won't cross paths again."

"She's a good artist and highly successful, which made her instant friends with Vivian. Vivian shows Camilla's art in her galleries. Camilla is good at what she does. Her art is bringing in higher returns and it's selling better than ever."

Noah was glad for her. She'd always been talented. But enough talk about Camilla. He changed the subject quickly, before Mike could go on about the woman. "Speaking of a wedding, too bad Jake won't be out of the military and back for your wedding."

"We waited for you. I'm not waiting another month for Jake to get back, even though I count him as a close friend," Mike said.

"I'm sure he'll understand."

"He won't care if he isn't in a wedding except that he'll miss a party. Jake loves a party."

After reminiscing a bit about their good friend and Ranger buddy Jake Ralston, Mike asked after Noah's plans now that he was home.

"I'll stay in Dallas for the next month to get business taken care of, see my family some, and I have Thane's gift to Camilla to deliver. Eventually, I'll go back to my West Texas Bar G Ranch."

"That's the best possible plan," Mike said, smiling. "If you want to buy a really fine horse, come by our place."

"I'll do that. When is a good time?"

Mike shrugged. "With our wedding coming up this weekend, either come out today or tomorrow or wait a couple of weeks until we return from our honeymoon."

"Thanks, Mike. I'll give you a call or text when I'm ready."

"Great. You know where the ranch is. Stay for dinner and get to know Vivian if you can."

"Thanks," he said and Mike nodded.

As the hour passed, they finished lunch and finally said goodbye. Noah left, thinking again about delivering the gifts from Thane. When he sat in his car, he called a phone number he still could remember easily and drew a deep breath as he waited to hear Thane's sister, Camilla Warren, answer.

Camilla

Camilla's heart skipped a beat when she looked at the name on the caller ID. Noah. She hadn't talked to him since the two weeks he'd been home on a furlough. Since they'd made a baby together. Sex with Noah had always been fabulous. In bed, they were compatible, in sync. Not so much out of the bedroom. A relationship between them never would have lasted. And now he would never forgive her deception.

She stared at the caller ID while the music on her phone continued to play, indicating an incoming call. She didn't want to answer. She and Noah had nothing to talk about and he should know that she would not go out with him. She couldn't imagine he would want to ask her out after the harsh words they'd had when they last parted. She didn't want to see him and she didn't want to talk to him.

His call kicked over to voice mail and minutes later her heart skipped another beat when she listened to Noah's familiar voice.

"Camilla, your brother has a gift for you. It's important because he went through hell—" Noah paused and tears stung her eyes because she loved her older brother and she knew Noah and Thane had been close friends since they had been in middle school.

She could hear Noah take a deep breath. "Thane went through hell to make sure I knew what he wanted. I promised him I would give a package to you. He was insistent I put it in your hand myself. Sorry Mike could have given it to you, but that wasn't what your brother wanted. This was a final request of a dying buddy, a man whose memory I will always honor, and I'm going to keep my promise to him and put his gift into your hand as he asked. Also, he gave me a present for your baby, his first nephew. I'm to give that present to him. I'll call again for a time." There was a brief pause, and then he added, "It's Noah, by the way."

She heard the click and dropped her phone to cover her face with her hands and sob for the big brother who had been killed, a brother who had been a friend and a second dad. He wasn't coming home. And she knew she was also crying over Noah, the man she had once loved with all her heart. The man she had to keep out of her life at all costs. Yet now there was a reason she had to see him, because she could not refuse her brother's dying request, either.

Thane had known she couldn't refuse to see Noah. Too easily, she could imagine her brother's motive in getting Noah to deliver the present to her. Even from the grave, he was taking charge of someone else's life. This time, hers. Thane was determined that Noah learn about Ethan. After the baby was born, Thane had written her and asked if Ethan was Noah's. He was the only person who had come up with the truth. She couldn't write back and admit it, though. Just the fact that she'd stalled had given him an answer. And then he'd gotten a call through to her and they had argued about it.

Thane tried almost as much as her dad to take charge of everything in his life. But he couldn't convince Camilla to tell Noah the truth.

She sighed as she wiped her eyes and tried to regain her composure. She would have to see Noah and accept her brother's present. To do so, they should make arrangements to meet as soon as possible and get it over and done. But she was not going to let him see Ethan. Noah could give her Ethan's present. Her son wouldn't know what was going on, anyway.

She picked up the phone to send a text to invite

Noah to come by. She had no intention of telling Noah ahead of time that Ethan would not be home. Noah would simply come another time. In minutes she received an answer and a time, which she accepted. She sighed as she wondered how she would get through seeing Noah tomorrow. Not only then, but at Vivian's wedding.

Vivian would marry Mike Moretti, another Ranger buddy and rancher who had been in Thane's outfit. Thane had hired Mike to replace their retiring foreman. Vivian knew about Camilla's breakup with Noah, so she had been sympathetic when she'd asked Camilla to be in her wedding, telling Camilla if she was uncomfortable accepting, she would understand. Camilla wanted to say no and stay far away, but she couldn't. For Thane's sake—and she truly liked Vivian—she would be in the wedding, which Vivian had originally said would be small with just family members and very close friends. That had changed because there were so many family members. Mike and Vivian both had brothers and close friends. One of Vivian's brothers would be best man. Noah would be a groomsman. Noah's sister, Stefanie, would be a bridesmaid.

Camilla hoped she could get through seeing Noah, talking to him, being in the wedding with him, without any tears. She was the one who had broken up the relationship and she thought by now she was over him, but hearing his voice not only made her cry, it made her weak in the knees and swamped her with longing to have his arms around her and to kiss him again—something she didn't want to feel. She had no future with Noah. Her feelings hadn't changed one tiny degree regarding his alpha-male ways. She just had to get through tomorrow's meeting and get through the wedding, and then Noah would be out of her life.

After the wedding, she didn't ever have to see Noah again. She would cling to that thought like a lifeline.

But first she had to make it through tomorrow.

The next day at noon her heart fluttered as she changed clothes for the third time. She shouldn't care how she looked or what she wore. She and Noah were finished forever and she would take the package and baby present her brother had sent and say goodbye and Noah would be gone. She lived in Dallas, and Noah lived two hundred and thirty miles away in West Texas on his Bar G Ranch. Now, if only her heart could get the message that seeing Noah wasn't important. Her heart was pounding, her hands were icy, her breathing was fast—why couldn't she get over him? She didn't want a future out on a ranch with a strong alpha male whose life choices were mostly the opposite of hers.

Annoyed by her reactions to seeing him, she took a deep breath.

Her door chimes made her jump and she realized how tense she was. She took another deep breath, glanced at herself in the mirror and shook her long, straight brown hair away from her face. Her gaze skimmed over her pale blue cotton blouse, matching slacks and high-heeled sandals. Then she hurried to the door, swinging it open and feeling her heart beat faster as she looked up into Noah's vivid blue eyes. In that instant, two years' worth of time vanished. In some ways it could have been yesterday when she'd last seen him. In other ways, change was evident. He looked older, taller, more broad-shouldered and even more incredibly handsome. His thick black hair was a mass of unruly curls above the most vivid blue eyes she had ever seen.

Looking like the rancher he was, Noah was in civilian clothes: fresh, dark jeans, a navy long-sleeved shirt and black boots. A short black beard was a new addition. He looked like a strong, handsome Texas cowboy, not a billionaire rancher and former officer of an elite military outfit. She couldn't speak and she wanted to walk into his arms and kiss him. She had thought she was getting over him, but the instant she looked into his eyes, such intense longing filled her that it hurt. For a moment they stared at each other and she realized he was as silent as she.

"Come in, Noah," she said quietly, her voice a whisper. Her pulse raced and she couldn't tear her gaze away from his. She couldn't move. Her heart pounded and she made an effort to step back so he could enter. When he did, she caught the scent of his aftershave. As he stepped in front of her, he paused to look down at her. She couldn't breathe while she wondered if he could hear her heart pound. He turned and walked on. Taking a deep breath, she closed the door and walked ahead of him into the living room.

"Where's your baby?" he asked, following her. "I expected you to be holding him."

"Actually, Noah, my mom came by and took Ethan with her. One of her friends is here from out of town and she wanted to show him off."

She entered her living room and turned to face him. He had a slight scowl and his gaze had grown cold.

"Camilla, I told you that I have Thane's gift to you and one to your son. What's his name—Ethan?"

"Yes—he's named for my uncle. I'm sorry," she answered, raising her chin, trying to get some force into her voice so she didn't sound guilty or intimidated. "I know you told me that you wanted to see Ethan, but this was special to Mom, and her friend will only be in town today. Besides, he's a baby," Camilla stated firmly and had a sinking feeling when his expression did not soften. "Ethan is fifteen months old. He won't know or care if you put that present in his little hands or not. That's ridiculous. He doesn't even know how to open a present. He'll probably chew on it. I'll get it to him and put it into his hands." Changing her tone, she waved her hand. "Have a seat, Noah, and relax," she said, motioning toward an armchair.

Noah shook his head. "Thanks, Camilla, but I have other places to go."

Why did his words hurt? He was stiff, cold and angry. She didn't want to react to him, to ache to be in his arms and to remember far too vividly his kisses.

"Do I get my present?" she asked.

He crossed the room and she couldn't resist letting her gaze flick over him. Her pulse raced as she noted differences. He stopped a couple of feet in front of her. Her gaze lowered to his mouth and she couldn't get her breath. She realized how she stared and her gaze flew up to meet his, and for a few seconds, she saw scalding desire, a hungry look that made her weak in the knees. She was the one who broke up with him, so why was she about to go up in flames just facing him now?

She fought to regain her composure, or at least feign it. Searching for something to say, she came up with a lame comment. "I think you're taller, Noah."

"I am," he answered. "I got measured enough in the Army to know I'm taller than when I went in. Taller, heavier, stronger and hopefully tougher. We'll see the next time I participate in a rodeo." He reached out, holding a package. "Here's your present from Thane, Camilla. He had very specific instructions for me."

Momentarily lost in thoughts about her brother, she accepted the small package and ran her hand over the ripped and wrinkled brown paper, tied tightly with twine. She thought about Thane, dying in Afghanistan, so far from home and family, having a present for her and one for Ethan. "Thank you. I'm glad you and Mike and Jake were with him. He died doing what he wanted," she said and stopped talking for a moment because tears threatened. "When I kissed him goodbye, I wondered if I would ever see him again," she whispered and turned her back to wipe her eyes. She tried to get her emotions under control and shifted her thoughts to Noah and the present, turning back to face him.

"Sorry, Noah. Thane was really special."

"Yes, he was. He was special to all of us under his command."

She took a deep breath. "You did what he wanted. I'll tell Ethan, when he's old enough to understand that Thane very specifically wanted you to bring his present home and he wanted you to place it in Ethan's hands yourself."

"And that's what I intend to do. I'll have to come back," he said, and she could hear the reluctance in his voice.

A chill slithered down her spine because she knew Noah would do whatever he said he would. She knew far too well how tough and unyielding he could be when he thought he was right.

"Noah, you're busy. I'm busy. Ethan is a baby and Thane wasn't thinking about how little Ethan is."

"Camilla," Noah said in such a cold voice that she stopped talking instantly. "Thane knew exactly what he was doing and saying. Those were the words of a dying man giving his last wishes. I promise you, your brother's thoughts were clear, and with great effort and some of his last breaths, he made me promise to put that gift into your baby's hands. He specifically said to not give it to you."

She felt heat rise in her face. She loved her brother, but he had always meddled in her life. This was why she wouldn't tie her life to a man who was an alpha male through and through. Her controlling brother had even managed to wring promises from his men that would bring about the results Thane wanted. He was just as bad as her father.

Her father had never been deeply interested in his kids. Early on, Thane took over being a second dad to her and sometimes he'd interfered in her life if he'd thought it was best.

She smiled sweetly. "All right, Noah. You can give the present to Ethan personally. I'll call you. It won't be this week because we have commitments, but next week should work."

Noah nodded. "If possible, as soon as you can. I want to get this done. I gave your brother my word that I would."

"Sure. You want to get back to your ranch, don't you?"

"You can't imagine how much I want to. It's been two years since I even saw it, back when I was on that furlough. You should have come out there with me at least once, Camilla. It's beautiful."

She shivered. "Noah, I've told you—we used to go see my grandparents on their ranch and it was never beautiful. It was scary and had snakes. I was bitten once, but it wasn't a poisonous one. My grandfather spent his time and money gambling and that ranch was insignificant to him. So were his grandkids. I hated it, and after my grandmother died, my grandfather let everything go. The house was dark and depressing. I told you—that's where my little brother, Winston, drowned. Our grandfather let us play on a frozen pond and the ice cracked. We all went in and that icy water was terrifying and I had nightmares about it for a couple of years. Thane pulled Winston out. He was only four. He got pneumonia and died. I've told you before."

"Yeah, I've heard Thane talk about it. That doesn't mean all ranches are dark, dangerous, gloomy and sad. That was your grandfather's doing."

"I'll agree with you on that one."

A faint smile raised one corner of his mouth. "Something we finally agree on."

"I've lost two brothers and an uncle because of accidents or violence. At least you can take care of yourself. When we were dating, maybe I should have gone to your ranch with you and you should have gone to an opera with me."

"I can't recall being invited to an opera."

"You would have turned me down."

Again, she saw a faint, crooked smile. "You should have tried me, Camilla. You'll never know whether I would have or wouldn't have."

They looked at each other and she felt that same pull, the attraction that was as intense as it had been when they dated. He had the most vivid blue eyes she had ever seen and they held her captive right now while her heart pounded. She couldn't breathe, couldn't look away and couldn't move.

"I'll see you next week," he said gruffly. But as his gaze lingered on her for a minute after he spoke, longing swamped her. She could just reach out and pull him back into her life. That thought came and immediately she stepped away from him. He might not ever want to be in her life again and she didn't want him back. He hadn't changed; he'd still try to run everything. Just like Thane. She knew Thane had been trying to get them together again or he would never have sent a present for Ethan and asked Noah to place it in Ethan's hands.

"I'll call you before I come out," Noah added, still standing in the same spot and looking at her.

Just as she'd expected, he turned the tables on her, taking charge of their next meeting. "Please do call. My schedule varies from week to week. I have a painting I'm working on."

"I'll call. You look great, Camilla," he said and his voice suddenly had a rasp that made her pulse jump. His gaze ran briefly over her from head to toe and back to look into her eyes. He might as well have run his fingers over her. She tingled from his glance—a mere glance—and she reacted to him.

"Thank you. So do you," she said in a voice that was almost a whisper.

"I don't know why in hell you fell in love with me

when you knew from day one the things I like and do, the kind of man I am," he said. His eyes blazed with anger and a muscle worked in his jaw.

Her temper flared over his comment and she leaned closer to him, as she breathed deeply and looked at his mouth. "Oh, I think you know full well why I fell in love with you," she said, reacting with anger and longing. Her emotions were raw and she hurt and was angry with him, while at the same time, she couldn't stop wanting him, his kisses and his arms around her.

Annoyed with Noah and herself, she slipped her arm around his neck, standing on tiptoe to kiss him, running her tongue slowly over his lips for seconds before his mouth opened on hers. His arm banded her waist tightly, yanking her against him, and he leaned over her, kissing her, thrusting his tongue over hers. It was a hot, demanding kiss that made her heart pound while she moaned with pleasure and forgot momentarily all their differences.

Abruptly he swung her up and released her. Both of them gasped for breath as they stared at each other. "Well, I knew there had to be some reason you liked me. That one hasn't changed. It's a package deal— it's all of me, the bossy male, the rancher, the cowboy and rodeo rider, the pilot." He glared at her and her heart still pounded. "I should go," he said.

He turned and left, walking toward his black sports car. She watched as he walked away with purpose, standing straight, looking like a soldier, someone who was accustomed to walking with shoulders back and chin up.

"The truth is, you don't want to change," she said softly, knowing he was out of earshot and couldn't possibly hear her. "You're not going to see Ethan," she whispered. "Not next week or next month or next year. Thane was meddling in my life, doing what he thought was best because he loved both of us, but it wasn't best for any of us—not for me, not for you and not for Ethan."

Her conscience hurt when she remembered Thane's call to her, the heated arguments between them— something she'd never had before in her life—and now her brother was gone and she wanted to say she was sorry she had argued with him. She wasn't sorry for what she had done and was still doing, but she was sorry she had fought with the brother she loved so much.

She had told him that she had rights and he was butting into something that was none of his business and could hurt three people.

He had told her what she was doing was wrong and Noah had legal rights that she was violating. Thane had said she should rethink what she was doing before she hurt three people badly.

She thought about Noah and whispered to him even though he had driven away. "You can keep Thane's present to Ethan. It won't be half as impor- tant as keeping you from giving it to him. If the day ever comes when you see Ethan, the moment you do, you'll know you're looking at your son. And if that happens, all hell will break loose between us, Noah Grant."

Three

Noah

As Noah drove away, he took deep breaths and relaxed his grip on the steering wheel. It had hurt far more than he had expected to see Camilla again. He thought he was getting over her, but the minute she opened the door, he knew damn well he hadn't gotten over her at all. He had just been busy trying to stay alive and do his job.

While he hurt, he wished he didn't care. He and Camilla had no future together and he didn't want to see her again because today had torn him up. She hadn't looked happy, either.

She had been prettier than ever, looking gorgeous, and his knee-jerk reaction had been to want to wrap her in his arms and kiss her for the next hour and carry her to bed.

He couldn't ever do that again.

He struck the steering wheel with his hand. He needed to get to the ranch and outside where he had hard, physical work. The Army was over. His life with Camilla was over. He had to move on and get a new life and try to forget her.

He hadn't helped himself by asking her why she fell in love with him when he knew what she liked and they both were tense and angry. Her kisses made him want to promise to change, to do whatever she wanted, but he hung on to his wits enough to know that he couldn't stop being decisive, controlling, demanding. He loved the Bar G Ranch and didn't want to give up that life. He'd lived in Dallas and worked in the family business and he'd had more of that than he wanted. That wasn't the life for him.

He drove carefully because he was upset and his mind was elsewhere. It was not until he was in his own condo that he could let go, let the memories that tugged at him come, the regrets, the anger, the longing he couldn't control.

He brewed coffee, poured a mug and went out on his balcony to look over the city of Dallas. He was high enough up that the horns and clatter of trucks were muffled.

He sat and sipped his coffee and thought about what else he had to do before he went back to the ranch, yet every few minutes, his thoughts would return to Camilla. He had to let go because they would not get back together. The differences were too big, too basic. She felt he was too strong an alpha male, making decisions and taking charge, because she had grown up with two take-charge males—Thane and her dad. She said her mother had given in to her dad always. Noah felt certain that wouldn't happen with Camilla. She was about as strong-willed as he was if she stopped to think about it. Would she really have liked him better if he couldn't take charge, couldn't make decisions and act on them? He didn't think so.

She hated her grandfather's ranch, thus she disliked all ranches. He knew her memories were terrible at her grandfather's place because her little brother had caught pneumonia from his fall into an icy pond and had later died. That would be a bad memory, but Noah didn't think his ranch would trigger any such memories. He should have tried more to coax her out to his ranch.

She loved life in the city. He loved it out on his ranch, which she had never even visited. They weren't going to work through their differences because neither of them would change. In bed was the one place where they had absolutely no disagreements. She was fantastic, instantly and intensely responsive. He sipped his coffee and made an effort to get his thoughts off sex with Camilla. The big deal was to give Camilla's baby his little present. Why the hell Thane had been so insistent on placing that present in his little nephew's hands, Noah couldn't imagine, unless it had been that the little kid had no dad and Thane hoped Noah would be enough interested in the child to try to work things out with Camilla.

Noah had always wondered if she'd married on the rebound because it had been so fast, coming up right after he had been home on furlough and they had gone another—and final—round in their battle over his alpha-male, take-charge way, their city versus country life.

A part of him suspected that Thane wanted them back together and thought her fatherless child might draw them closer. That wasn't going to happen. Noah knew Camilla hadn't changed. She didn't want any part of him in her life.

He sipped his hot coffee, closing his eyes, lost in memories of holding and kissing her that he couldn't push out of mind. She was still the sexiest woman he had ever known. She dazzled him, and until he'd left for the Army, they'd had fun together. He had been staying in Dallas some of the time, or coming in from the ranch often to take her out, and for a time, they seemed to be getting closer. Until he started inviting her to his ranch.

Give the baby his present and tell her goodbye. After that and Mike's wedding, there won't be any other reason to try to see her.

His logical mind gave him clear commands, but he couldn't stop the memories that clutched at his heart. Memories of one of the last times they were together, when he invited her to his ranch and she turned him down, leading to an argument as he tried to talk her into coming for a weekend. Finally he had stepped closer to slip his arms around her.

"Here's where all our arguments vanish," he'd said quietly. His mouth had covered hers and his tongue had gone deep while he kissed her. He'd held her close against him with one arm, his other hand slipping lightly over her curves, sliding down over her trim bottom, and then he'd shifted, his hand drifting beneath her dress to caress her breast. She'd been soft, wonderful, sweet-smelling, absolute temptation. He'd been lost. Her softness had made him shake.

For a moment she'd stood still in his arms, but with a moan, her arms had circled his neck and she'd thrust her hips against him, clinging tightly to him as she kissed him passionately in return, and he hadn't wanted to ever stop.

He'd leaned over her, pouring himself into the kiss as if he could kiss away her reluctance and make her want a life together. Make being with him more important to her than her dislike of country life and her views on alpha males. Their moments of intimacy were the best possible, but it always came back to the truth: he couldn't change the kind of man he was and make false promises that he never could keep and he didn't want to give up his ranch. City life wasn't for him.

Shifting, he'd slipped his hand beneath her dress, caressing her silken thighs so lightly, hearing her moan as she moved against him. Then he'd forgotten all their harsh words and impossible goals as he leaned down again to kiss her.

"I want you, Camilla," he'd whispered minutes later, running his hand lightly over her nape and then holding her close.

She'd inhaled, closing her eyes to kiss him in return. She'd moaned softly and run both hands down his sides. "Noah, this isn't going to solve anything."

"Shh. For a few minutes shut out the world. We'll talk about it later."

"That just means you're going to do what you wa—"

He'd kissed her so she would stop talking and there were no arguments. The sex had been hot, irresistible, and he'd picked her up to carry her to bed, where they forgot their differences.

Hours later, he'd slipped out of bed, gathering his clothes to shower and dress. When he'd come out, she'd been waiting. She had showered, pulled on jeans and a blue T-shirt.

They'd faced each other in silence. "We didn't solve one thing. You just took charge and swept us into making love."

"It looks as if we're caught up in irreconcilable differences because I can't stop being an alpha male. And frankly, I don't want to give up living on my ranch. That's my life."

"And I don't want to leave the city life. Noah, why are we even arguing? You haven't proposed. We're not that deeply involved."

"One of us was," he'd said. "All right, Camilla. I guess we say goodbye. I'm going to the military, anyway. I won't be around for a few years."

She'd flinched and drawn a deep breath. "We're just opposites and neither one of us wants to change."

"I guess you're right. One goodbye kiss," he'd said, kissing her again, knowing he had lost her. Hurting, getting aroused again, he'd held her tightly and they'd kissed.

He'd released her abruptly and stepped back, clenching his fists so he wouldn't pick her up and carry her to bed. "This is goodbye. It's what you want. Not what I want. You're very special, Camilla. I am who I am and I guess you can say the same about yourself. You fuss about your brother being an alpha male, as well as your dad, but that didn't stop you from loving Thane and turning to him when you had a problem. Aw, hell. There's too much about me you don't like—too much you love that I don't want any part of, like living in the city and working here. I'm here now more than I want to be so I can take you out. Well, that's over. I'm going into the Army and I'll be gone. We just said goodbye."

Tears had spilled over and run down her cheeks, but her frown had kept him from closing the space between them to take her into his arms.

"You're right, Noah. I don't want to live on a ranch or in the country. You're a strong man and you'll always want life your way."

When he'd started to reply, she'd held up her hand as if to stop him. "I know what you're about to say—

that I have a strong, take-charge tendency myself. Maybe so. We're opposites in too many ways. All we have that goes smoothly is sex. That's breathtaking. But there's more to life than that. We have to get out of bed, and from the moment we do, we're opposites. So I guess it is goodbye," she'd said, wiping her eyes.

"You know how I feel about you, but I have to be honest and I have to be me."

He'd turned and walked out of her condo, knowing it was the end of their relationship and wondering how long it would take him to end his feelings for her.

The memory faded, but instead of feeling like three years ago, the pain of that breakup and goodbye was fresh. His feelings for her hadn't ended as he had thought they would when he was on active duty. He'd thought he was getting over her and then one glimpse of her set him back. There was one ray of hope for getting past the hurt from their breakup—he had done far better when he was away from her.

As soon as he delivered her baby's present and was in Mike Moretti's wedding, he would rarely ever see her. Thane was gone now, so his friendship with her brother could no longer throw them together. He planned to stay in Dallas for several weeks to be close to his dad. He would have to come and go from the ranch and spend more time in the city than he had originally expected.

There hadn't been a beautiful, fun, sexy woman in his life since he went into the Army. If he found one, maybe he could move on completely and the hurt over Camilla would lessen and disappear.

Convincing himself that life would improve, he tried to focus on the things he needed to get done while he was in Dallas. He needed to go see his dad. After that, he wanted to go by the family's commercial real-estate business. The company headquarters of Grant Realty was in downtown Dallas, which was run by Ben, and they had two suburban offices covering the metropolitan area of Dallas and Fort Worth, Eli running one of those and Stefanie managing the other.

And he also needed to deal with Thane's final wishes. Camilla ought to have her baby home and available for him to visit early next week. Before that, Noah would see her in Mike's wedding because he would be a groomsman and he knew she would be one of the bridesmaids, and then Camilla would be out of his life. They would be finished and he could say goodbye and, hopefully, forget her.

The next morning when Noah stopped at the back of the house, his parents were sitting in big rocking chairs on the veranda. He joined them and sat talking, taking his time and enjoying the morning, seeing his folks and gazing at their yard filled with flowers, a lily pond with a waterfall and fountains. He knew that around the corner on the east side of the house, there was another large veranda with an outdoor living room and kitchen. Beyond it was a sparkling swimming pool with more waterfalls and fountains.

"Let's go to my office," his dad said, and Noah nodded, strolling slowly beside his dad through the hall to the large home office. Cal Grant entered and crossed the room to sit in the big leather recliner he'd had for years. Noah turned to close the door and then sat in a hard, wooden rocking chair.

"I remember when your feet didn't touch the floor when you'd sit in that chair," his dad said, smiling at him.

"Yeah. I remember sitting here getting lectures about my behavior," Noah replied, and his dad chuckled.

"They must have done some good. You turned out to be a good man."

Noah looked into his dad's eyes. "Ben told me about your heart attacks and your bypass surgery, Dad. I wish I could do something."

"This came sooner than I thought something would, but I'm doing okay. I walk on a treadmill some, try to eat right. I feel okay."

"That's good news. I'm just sorry about what you've been through and that I wasn't here."

"You were doing a service for me and for all of us. Your mother is in a dither over this, so the less said around her the better. I feel better now that you're home. That's good."

"It's good to be home."

"You'll be going to your ranch soon."

He nodded. "I have Mike Moretti's wedding to Vivian Warner coming up and I'll be around here for a while after that. We'll get to see each other."

"Noah, you faced that you might not return when you enlisted. With old age, it's a given. We have trusts set up, the business is taken care of and I'm out of it. I've had a really good life. Financially, there shouldn't be any problem or even responsibility for your mom. Harvey's been our accountant for years and he'll handle things. If something happens to me, just give her your love and attention the way you always have. Take care of Mom and try to not grieve. I've had a good life."

"There's no way in hell anyone can avoid grief. Not when you love someone," Noah replied, not wanting to even contemplate losing his father. Surprisingly, another thought entered his mind. Camilla. He wondered if he was going to miss her for the rest of his life, too.

He leaned toward his dad. "If there is anything I can do to make life easier, you tell me. Would you mind if I go to one of your doctor's appointments with you? I'd like to meet and talk to your doctor."

"I knew you would," his dad said. "Look on my desk. I wrote the names and numbers of all the docs I've seen. Feel free to call and talk to them. I told them you probably would when you came home. Also, you can look at my calendar on the desk and see my appointments. I'd be happy for you to go along."

"Thanks," Noah said, getting up to walk to his dad's desk.

"Are you seeing Camilla now?"

"No, sir, that's over. It was over before I enlisted."

"Sorry, son. She seemed nice and we've missed seeing her, but some things just don't work out. We were saddened over Thane and we're both glad you're home. You've served and Mother needs you. We're both going to need you this year."

"Yes, sir, I'll be here, and you call anytime you need me no matter what hour it is. I've got a pilot's license and my own plane. I can get here from the ranch easily in no time."

"Thanks. I'll do that."

"I better run, Dad. You'll see me a lot now that I'm home and especially when I'm in Dallas," Noah said and realized he might have to rethink the time he intended to spend on his ranch. "For now I've got some time, so I'm staying in the city."

"Good. We're always glad to see you, but don't stay on my account. I'm getting along fine." His dad stood and they faced each other.

Noah stepped up to wrap his arms around his dad and hug him lightly, realizing how frail his father had become. "Life is tough, Dad," he whispered.

"Yeah," his dad answered. "So are you." They stepped away and his father placed his hand on Noah's shoulder. "You'll do what you have to do and do it well. You always have."

"Thank you," Noah answered. "I had a good teacher."

They smiled at each other and turned for the door that Noah stepped forward to open.

Noah's mother had been sitting where she could see them and she stood to walk into the hall. "Can you stay?"

"I have to go now, Mom. I'll be in touch and you call me whenever you want. I'm close and I can get here easily."

"Thanks, Noah. You come home when you can. We're so glad you're back and we want to see you."

"Thanks," he said, opening the door to go out the back steps. They followed and stood on the veranda as he crossed the shady drive to his car.

He climbed in, waved and drove away, wondering how well his dad really was. He glanced at the time. He had a few errands to run, but his mind wasn't really on those tasks. Instead, he thought of Camilla. The mere mention of her name conjured up memories of kisses, stirring desire and lusty thoughts that were unwanted. How long would it take him to forget her once he walked away this time?

And why did that prospect hurt so much?

Four

Camilla

Friday afternoon before Camilla had to dress for the rehearsal dinner and party Mike and Vivian were having, she picked up Thane's letter and stood looking at the envelope.

She had put off reading it because she knew it would hurt and she would miss Thane more than ever. Also, she suspected he would try to explain why he had asked Noah to personally deliver her present and Ethan's. She didn't want to read a letter from her beloved brother urging her to marry Noah. It had been a few days now since she had seen Noah and she hadn't called him about Ethan. She was certain when she saw him tonight at the rehearsal dinner he would ask her about Ethan and she could say she forgot.

She propped Thane's letter on a vanity, running her hand over it again because it was a tie to her brother, something he had sent to her, written, handled, wrapped for her, and it seemed a tiny part of him. "You should have stayed home the way Vivian and I wanted you to," she whispered, closing her eyes.

She opened her eyes and turned her back on Thane's letter. She might read it after the wedding when she wouldn't see any more of Noah. At least that was what she hoped. Noah could be mule-stubborn. At the thought that he wouldn't give up seeing Ethan, a chill slithered over her and she shivered. She had to keep Noah away from Ethan. She was doing something she shouldn't, but she still wasn't ready to share her son and she didn't want to marry Noah solely because of Ethan. They had too much between them to make a relationship work out of obligation alone.

She turned and looked at the dress hanging in her closet, eager to get out of the funk that thoughts of her late brother and Noah had put her in. Festive and lively, the sleeveless dress was a scarlet red with a scoop neckline and a straight skirt ending above her knees.

Mike and Vivian would have the rehearsal at the church and then the wedding party would go to a downtown club for dinner. As Camilla dressed, her thoughts of Noah returned. She had mixed feelings. She dreaded seeing him because she hadn't called him to come give Thane's gift to Ethan. The last time with Noah had been painful and she didn't want another confrontation. Also, when they were together, there had been fireworks with hot kisses. She had dreamed about him every night.

Within days he would vanish out of her life. She would not tie her life to a strong alpha male, especially one who liked the opposite of most things that she liked. On one of life's most basic needs—where to live—they were poles apart. Noah would have all sorts of ideas about raising Ethan and she suspected they would battle each other at every turn. She didn't want his interference with her baby.

Their baby.

At the thought, a twinge of guilt disturbed her, but she tried to focus on the wedding and think about her friends that she would see tonight. At the same time, excitement skittered over her nerves and she could not get Noah out of her thoughts. Underneath all her dread was a thrill at seeing him again that she couldn't shake and didn't want to feel. When—and how—would she get over Noah?

She was still asking herself that question when she got to the church.

The wedding party met there to run through what everyone would do at the upcoming ceremony. When Camilla stepped out of her car, she glanced at a black sports car pulling in at the end of the row. In seconds Noah stepped out and in a few more seconds she would catch up with him.

In a navy suit and white shirt, with a black Western

hat and black boots, he looked incredibly handsome.
Her heart thudded as he faced her, and she was glad
he couldn't know how her pulse raced.

Noah

When he saw Camilla, he drew a sharp breath. In
high heels, and a sexy red dress that showed a lot of
her gorgeous long legs, she looked incredible. With
each step she took, her silky hair swung across her
shoulders. While his pulse raced, he couldn't stop
looking at her. As he stared and walked toward her,
she smiled faintly, her full rosebud lips curving as
if in an invitation. He wanted to walk up to her, put
his arms around her and kiss her. His heart pounded
while he clenched his fists and reminded himself that
she was off-limits and out of his life. She would not be
seated by him, nor would she do anything with him
tonight. If he didn't want to hurt more than ever, he
would stay away from her.

Mike had called to ask if he wanted to be seated
with Camilla, and Noah told him no, that it was definitely over between them.

As she neared, he smiled. "You look stunning,"
he said and meant it. His voice had a raspy sound
because he was aroused. He wanted to whisk her off
somewhere they could be alone, where he could hold
and kiss her and just look at her. She took his breath
away and he knew the luscious curves beneath that
dress.

She smiled slightly in return, but her hazel eyes were cold. "Thank you, Noah. You look very handsome."

"Thanks, Camilla," he said, falling into step beside her. "I'll ask now before we get involved in the wedding. You were going to call me about bringing Thane's present to your son."

She shook her head. "Noah, sorry. I'm busy right now. It's been a hectic summer. I'm sorry I didn't get to call you, but when I'm home and see my calendar, I'll call this week. You said you'd be in Dallas awhile," she said.

"I'll expect to hear from you this week. I want to get this done."

"I understand and I'll call you."

He reached out to get the door, but he didn't open it for her. With wide eyes she looked up and his heart pounded.

"You really do look gorgeous," he repeated softly, aching to touch her.

"Thank you again," she whispered.

His heartbeat raced as he gazed down at her and remembered her kisses the last time they had been together. His heart pounded. How was he going to get over her?

"We better go inside," she said, smiling at him.

"You're right," he replied and opened the door for her. After she entered, he followed her in and then went the opposite direction so he could let his heartbeat slow and his temperature cool.

Camilla

Camilla glanced over the people standing in clusters in the foyer. She spotted Vivian and headed toward her. She couldn't resist glancing over her shoulder and saw Noah with his back to her, talking to Stefanie Grant, his younger sister. Camilla's heart was still racing from just walking past him through the open door as he held it for her. When she had, she'd caught the faint scent of his aftershave that triggered memories of when they'd kissed. She remembered the feel of his slightly rough stubble against her face and his strong arms around her. After this wedding it might be life without Noah in it. Just the thought hurt, yet she couldn't change her mind. No matter how much she missed him, wanted him, dreamed about him, she couldn't deal with his strong alpha ways and his cowboy lifestyle out on a ranch.

Smiling, Vivian looked radiant, and Camilla remembered Vivian had that same radiance when she had married Thane. Thane had looked as if he was the happiest man on the planet and Vivian had looked as if she adored her new husband. Camilla hurt for losing her brother, as well as losing Vivian in the family.

Wearing a pink suit with a sparkling diamond necklace, Vivian hugged Camilla. "You look great tonight. I love your dress."

"Thanks. You look beautiful and I'm happy for you. Everyone says Mike is a great guy."

"I think so," Vivian said, her eyes twinkling.

Camilla's smile vanished and she touched Vivian's wrist lightly. "I know you're supremely happy, but I also know this has to have moments that are hard for you."

"A little," Vivian admitted, "but I'm marrying a man who is as understanding as your brother was. I can't believe I've found two of them. Well, Thane found Mike for me. He is understanding and it takes away a ton of sadness. I'm so happy and we're happy," she said as she glanced across the room at Mike again and back to Camilla.

Camilla felt her insides clutch. Would she ever find that kind of happiness with someone? A dull ache enveloped her as she looked around.

In that moment, Camilla realized Vivian might have been a closer friend if she had tried to get to know her more. She regretted she hadn't because Thane had loved her, and the little Camilla had been around Vivian, she had liked her, too. She and Vivian both shared a common bond of being artists.

"I'm happy for both of you and I'm certain this is what my oldest brother wanted to have happen. He was always trying to take care of everybody, sometimes to the point of meddling in lives," she said, and Vivian's smile broadened.

"Yes, he did, and he had an uncanny way of being right about what he thought everyone should do," Vivian replied. "He chose well. Mike is a great guy. Camilla, when things settle after the wedding and honeymoon, I expect us to still get together over our art and I want to keep showing your paintings in my galleries."

"Thanks, Vivian. That's good to know."

"I'm glad your other brothers could get here for the wedding. They're already here. I've talked to them," she said and looked around as Camilla did.

"Ahh, excuse me. Mike is motioning and he's with the minister, so we're probably getting ready for the rehearsal. The sooner we do that, the sooner we can go to dinner."

"Of course," Camilla answered and watched Vivian walk away. She was certain Thane had sent Mike home not only to run the Tumbling T ranch, but also to meet and marry Vivian. She was equally certain her brother had wanted Noah to get back with her. She sighed. That would not happen.

"Hello, little sis." She turned to face her two older brothers, Mason and Logan. She hugged Logan, gazing into hazel eyes like her own. He was thirty, single, and they saw each other often in Dallas events. He liked the same things she did and both had season tickets to the symphony and to the Dallas operas. They both knew Noah was the father of her child, but unlike their oldest brother, Logan and Mason were willing to let her live her life her way, and they respected her choices, for which she was grateful to both of them.

In spite of that, it was Thane she had always felt the closest to and had confided in as a child.

Mason gave her a quick hug and smiled. Mason

looked more like their dad with brown eyes and blond hair.

"I want to come see my little nephew while I'm home. I don't want him to forget me."

She smiled. "He won't forget you and we'll be glad to see you."

"That includes me, too," Logan said.

"You both are welcome anytime. Just let me know to make sure we're there."

She knew her brothers—they came alone to the rehearsal dinner, but each one would probably leave with a pretty woman.

Shortly, they went through the rehearsal. She was paired with one of Mike's brothers, Tony Moretti, and Noah was with one of Vivian's unmarried friends, a tall, striking redhead named Mia Mason.

As she chatted with various members of the wedding party, she turned to face Stefanie, Noah's sister. Stefanie smiled at her.

"Hi. I want to talk to you, Camilla. Maybe we have a minute now."

"Sure, Stefanie. What's up?" she asked, looking into another pair of thickly lashed vivid blue eyes. Stefanie's black hair was long and wavy, a tangle of silky strands. Noah's sister was beautiful with rosy cheeks, full red lips and a gorgeous figure. She seemed to have boundless energy and an optimistic outlook on life that Camilla envied. A fun person, Stefanie was more outgoing than her older brother and

Camilla enjoyed knowing her. Although she didn't know her well, they moved in the same social circles.

"I have a deal for you," Stefanie said, wasting no time. "We have some property in Chicago I've been working on and we just sold one of the smaller suburban buildings to a prestigious art gallery. We sold it to them before it ever went on the market and they got a good deal. They're extremely happy about it."

"Congratulations! That's quite a coup for you." Camilla smiled, surprised at Stefanie telling her all this.

"Thanks. They're thrilled and so grateful for letting them have an early shot at the space. The thing is, I showed them some of your landscapes and they loved them. I think they may contact you for a showing in their new gallery."

"Stefanie, that's fabulous," Camilla said, meaning it. "I'll let you know if I hear from them. Thank you. I'd love to have a showing in Chicago."

"I thought you would," Stefanie said. Something in her smile gave Camilla a thought. She wondered if Stefanie wanted her to spend time in Chicago in order to get her away from her brother and out of his life. She was doing that anyway, but she still was happy about the chance to showcase her art in Chicago.

"I'm excited over this. Is the name of this gallery secret for now? I know some of them."

When she looked down at the card in her hand, she gasped. "Stefanie," she said, smiling at Noah's sister, "I've been to this gallery—just to look—and I've seen their ads and a few lists of artists who have some showings there. This is fabulous. I can't thank you enough. This is wonderful."

"Don't get too excited until they actually call, or you can call them and see what happens," Stefanie said, smiling and sounding pleased. "Part of their interest in you is doing it as a thank-you to us for giving them an early chance to purchase the building, because it's a fabulous building in a great location. Part of it is your art. They liked your work, so good luck with it. Contact them and see what happens. You have nothing to lose."

"No, I don't. This is just marvelous. Does Noah know about this?"

"No. I thought the two of you—" She waved her hand.

"You're right. We're not seeing each other, but I wanted to make sure. I'm thrilled about this opportunity. Thank you for showing them my art."

"Glad to. I hear you're a mommy now. Congratulations. I'm sorry about the divorce, but I know you're happy with the little baby."

"I love him with all my heart," she said and gazed into Stefanie's blue eyes. A twinge of guilt filled her because she was keeping Stefanie from knowing her little nephew. "I'll let you know what happens. Thank you again."

"Good luck with it. I hope it goes really well," she said.

Camilla watched Stefanie walk away. Whatever Stefanie's motives, Camilla was thrilled over the prospect of getting a showing with that gallery. She slipped the card into a pocket in her dress.

To her relief, at dinner she was seated at the opposite end of the table from Noah, near Logan and Mason and between more of Mike's family. She did have a good time at moments, but she couldn't shake her awareness of Noah, and occasionally, she couldn't resist glancing his way. Three times he was looking right back at her, which startled her each time, and she could feel a flush crawl up her cheeks even after she had turned away. Once when she looked, his dark head was bent close to Mia Mason, who was laughing, and it hurt to see them having fun together.

Still, the prospect of getting more deeply involved with Noah wasn't appealing, either.

By ten o'clock, the party began to break up. She watched Noah leave with Mia and wondered if they were going out somewhere for a drink, going home together or if he was just walking her to her car. It hurt to think about him moving on, having a life with someone else in his arms, going out with another woman, marrying her. She gave herself a mental shake. She had to stop thinking about Noah.

It was easy to tell that to herself, impossible to do.

She glanced at Mike and Vivian, who were holding hands, smiling at each other, and she felt another pang. She was happy for them. Her brother had been on target on that one. Mike really was a great guy.

As she expected, Logan told her goodbye and left with one of the pretty bridesmaids.

Mason waved as he left and one of Vivian's pretty relatives was with him.

As she drove home, she wondered if Noah could be put off indefinitely about the gift for Ethan. He hadn't seemed too concerned tonight. But it wasn't like Noah to let something go, so she better start figuring out exactly what she was going to do. Guilt still nagged at her, but without a doubt Noah would want in his son's life.

When she arrived home, she talked to her nanny briefly before telling her goodbye and going to Ethan's room. She stood beside his crib, gazing down at him and brushing soft curls back from his forehead.

"I love you, my sweet baby. You look like your daddy," she said wistfully.

She thought of Noah and from out of nowhere came an errant thought. A wish that Noah was standing beside her and they could enjoy their son together.

She had no idea where that wish came from…but she knew it could only ever be that. A wish.

Five

Camilla

With a sigh and determined steps, she tiptoed out of the nursery and walked into her bedroom to pick up the box from her brother. She carried it to her rocker, kicking off her shoes and turning the box in her hands.

She tried to untie the twine. It took a long time and she rocked as she bent over it, determined to avoid cutting the twine he had used. She knew it was foolish, but she wanted to keep the box just the way it had been in Thane's hands. It was her last tie to her big brother. She missed him and it hurt unbearably. She looked at Ethan's picture, his smiling baby face, and love filled her, along with the knowledge that she would risk her life to save him if she had to. And she always felt gratitude for the men and women who served in the military to keep peace and America safe, even though she was thankful her other two brothers had not joined the military. Thane had been special, a brother and sometimes another dad to her. The thought of him dying from injuries in a foreign country hurt badly.

It took a long time, but she finally unwrapped the twine and then the paper around a box, constantly aware that it was last handled by her brother. The box contained something wrapped in more brown paper and beneath it a white envelope with her name scrawled across it. When she opened the brown paper wrapping, a bracelet of gold links fell out into her lap. She picked it up and slipped it on. It looked old in the soft light. She rubbed it against her cheek and wiped away tears as she picked up the envelope to find a letter.

Camilla,
If Noah brings this to you, then it's because I won't be coming home to you. Your worst fears for me came true. Even though I've made the ultimate sacrifice, if I had to make the choice again, I would still go into the service.

I hope your feelings change about Noah being a rancher. I've been to his ranch, and I promise you, it is not like our grandfather's ranch at all. Go and see for yourself. Noah is not a compulsive gambler as was Granddad, who paid no more attention to his ranch than he did to his grandkids, namely us. As for worrying about alpha males—you're a strong woman and can hold your own. You are closing yourself off from happiness. Don't shut your baby away from it. He should know his daddy.

I want you to know I will always love you, my baby sister. I wish I could see your little boy grow up and I wish I could be part of his life. I hope I have done some small part in keeping America safe for him to grow up in freedom the way we did.

My deepest brotherly love to you. Hug my little nephew for me. Please let him know the fine man and soldier who is his daddy. He needs his dad in his life. He needs both of you—a family like we had.

Here's a bracelet I bought. It's old, but pretty, and I thought of you.
Thane Warner, Captain, US Army Ranger

She put her head in her hands and cried. "I miss you," she whispered. Finally, she wiped away tears and folded the letter to put it back into the envelope. She stared into space as she contemplated her brother's words. She didn't know if she could ever tell Noah about his baby. If she did, it would turn both her life and Noah's upside down again and be another upheaval even bigger than when he enlisted. Guilt plagued her and she stared down at Thane's letter. She knew what he wanted her to do, but the minute she did, Noah would take charge and want to do things his way. And she couldn't allow that.

"I'm sorry, Thane. I can't do it," she whispered, tears falling again. She shook her head. "I just can't tell him. Ethan is a happy baby now even if he doesn't have a daddy," she whispered. "I can't deal with Noah taking over my life and Ethan's."

She stood to get ready for bed, her thoughts on Ethan. It was for the best that she avoid the man altogether. Then she realized what awaited her tomorrow. It was Vivian and Mike's wedding, which meant she would see Noah again.

The sunny day was perfect for a wedding. All the bridesmaids wore short, straight black dresses with white chiffon scarves at the vee necklines. As Camilla walked down the aisle, she glanced ahead. Mike and his groomsmen stood waiting and her gaze went to Noah, who was watching her from under his dark lashes. Her breath caught and pain squeezed her heart. Noah was more handsome than ever in a black tux. She once thought she'd walk down the aisle toward him as her groom.

At that lost dream she felt longing for Noah tug at her heart and looked away. But as she reached the point to turn to join the bridesmaids, she made a mistake and glanced at him again and her heart thudded. Nearly stumbling, she took her place and turned to watch the next bridesmaid come down the aisle. Mia's gaze was on Noah, too, as she walked.

In minutes Vivian came down the aisle. She looked radiant in a crepe sleeveless dress with a round neck and short, straight skirt. Camilla was happy for her and for Mike. Once again, Camilla was certain this was what Thane had wanted when he couldn't come home. If only Camilla could be so certain that her brother was right when it came to her.

For the first time, she gave some thought to what she was doing in keeping Ethan from knowing his dad. Was she cheating her baby out of a close, important relationship that would help him grow into the wonderful man his daddy was?

She barely heard the service for thinking about Noah and then it was time to process back up the aisle. All through the pictures she was conscious of Noah. He spent his time talking to Mia and Stefanie and then at the reception he was with Mia. Camilla stood watching him and thinking about Thane's letter. It was later in the evening when Mia finally moved away from Noah and Camilla crossed the room to talk to him.

"Noah, wait." He turned and her heart raced. Was she making the wrong decision for the wrong reasons? Was it Thane's letter or was it that she had lost Noah and she didn't want to let go? She couldn't answer her own questions.

She stood in front of him. "I can meet with you this

week if you want to give Ethan his present. I need to talk to you anyway."

"Good. How's Wednesday?"

"Wednesday's fine. I'd like to talk to you first, so can you come at about two because Ethan will be taking a nap then—at least, I hope he'll be."

"Sure," Noah answered. "I'll be there at two."

"Good. We need to do this before you leave for your ranch."

"Yes, we do, even though I'm not going as soon as I had originally planned."

"Well, I may not be here too long," she replied. "I don't know whether Stefanie told you or not, but she gave my name to an art gallery in Chicago. They contacted me today and offered me a showing, so I'll be going to Chicago soon. I've told Stefanie thanks because it's a wonderful opportunity."

"She didn't mention any of this to me, but that's good news for you."

"Also, that package you brought had a letter from Thane urging me to let you meet Ethan."

The corner of Noah's mouth lifted in a faint smile. "Thane was always arranging everything in his life and I'm sure he couldn't resist arranging his baby sister's, too."

Shaking her head, she smiled. "No, he could not." For a moment they were both silent. "Well, I'll see you Wednesday afternoon."

"Thanks, Camilla. I want to get this done and keep my promise."

"My meddling brother," she said, shaking her head as she walked away.

In her heart she wanted nothing more than to be here with Noah and to leave with him. But her head told her differently. The man had a love of everything country, wanted to be a rancher 24/7, had a need to take charge always. They were simply not compatible. Monday night she had tickets with a friend to the symphony. Tuesday, she had agreed to an appearance at an art gallery showing her work. That evening she was attending a charity dinner. Noah wouldn't want to be involved in any of those activities.

She hadn't slept much last night after she had read Thane's letter. His words had made her think. Was she cheating her baby out of knowing his dad? She hadn't really looked at it from her baby's standpoint until she read Thane's letter. Noah would be a wonderful dad; she had no doubt of that.

Her eyes sought him, and she saw him leaving with Mia. Pain stabbed her heart. Out of the corner of her eye she saw Stefanie, who was also watching Noah, and she saw the smile on her face as he left with Mia.

Maybe her earlier suspicion had been right. Stefanie had arranged for the Chicago contact to get Camilla out of town. Away from Noah. Still, it was a wonderful opportunity, one she intended to take full advantage of to further her career. Besides, she knew Noah and Stefanie were close and Stefanie probably was concerned about her brother and his happiness. She couldn't fault Stefanie for that.

Noah had a nice family. She had met all of them, been with them for parties and family gatherings. For the first time she realized she was keeping Ethan not only from his dad, but also his grandparents and aunts and uncles. And he was the first grandchild. Ben and Hallie did not have any children. Eli wasn't married and neither was Stefanie.

The thought stuck with her all the way home. When she got in, she dismissed the nanny and went to check on Ethan. Tenderly she touched his forehead as he slept. He looked so much like Noah. It was his blue eyes and black curly hair.

Tears ran down her cheeks. "I love you, Ethan," she whispered. And in that moment she knew that her son should know his daddy. She was cheating him out of a tie that was one of the most important in life.

She shut the nursery door and went into her bedroom, where she picked up Thane's letter, running her hand on the paper. "Thane, you sent Mike and Noah home with promises to you to do things here that you knew would change lives. But, as usual, you're right. Ethan should know his dad because Noah is a fine man and has a wonderful family. But I don't want to lose my baby doing this. Noah can be stubborn and hard." Tears stung her eyes and she covered her face to cry, shaking because she was so scared she would lose Ethan.

Noah would instantly step in and she would have to share Ethan almost immediately, so she'd better pull herself together and start thinking about what to do when she told him he had a son.

Was she going to be strong enough to do that?

Noah

Wednesday morning Noah felt he was beginning to fit back into his life as it was before he went into the Army. He knew his sister was matchmaking, but so far she was doing a good job of it. He liked Mia, he had fun when he was with her, but his mind still continued to drift to Camilla. It had hurt to watch her walk down the aisle and know that someday she would marry someone else. How long would it take him to get over her?

Sometimes he would see a tall woman with straight brown hair and he'd go out of his way until he could see whether or not it was Camilla.

He was glad she had set a time for him to deliver Thane's gift to his little nephew. He had expected to do that and then he would say a permanent goodbye to Camilla. Eventually, he would go to the ranch, where physical work would keep him busy, and he'd do better about getting over her. Now, because of his dad, he wanted to stay in Dallas longer, and seeing Mia a few times had helped a little.

For the twentieth time that morning, he checked his watch. It was hours yet before he'd go see Camilla. He had to bank his eagerness to see her and to stop checking the time, but he was so curious as to why she wanted to talk to him. He'd just have to wait to find out.

About midmorning he pulled into his parents' drive.

He went by to see them nearly every morning and often in the evening.

As long as he was in Dallas, he wanted to spend what time he could with them. He enjoyed his dad's company and Noah was glad that he had the chance to thank his dad for being the best father ever.

After visiting his parents, he stopped at Ben's office. Then, finally, at twenty minutes before two, he drove to Camilla's house. It was in a gated area with winding drives past elegant mansions with tall oaks casting cool shadows. Behind a high wrought-iron fence stood a large two-story colonial. Well-tended flower beds bordered the front porch. A splashing fountain was in the center of the circle drive. Her home was beautiful, which didn't surprise him. Her family was wealthy and he knew she had investments in family businesses. Plus, from what he'd heard, her art was bringing in more.

When Camilla swung open the door, his pulse jumped. In a blue T-shirt and tight jeans, she looked gorgeous. His reaction to seeing her was just as strong as it had been that first time after coming home from the Army.

"Come in, Noah," she said, stepping back.

Carrying the small parcel from Thane, Noah entered, following her into her living room, his gaze

on her tight jeans and trim butt as she walked ahead
of him. Once again, he realized he hadn't lost any of
his desire for her.

"Can I get you something to drink?" she asked,
turning to face him.

All he wanted to do was step closer, wrap his arms
around her and kiss her. Instead, he shook his head.
"Thanks. I'm fine."

"Have a seat. I want to talk to you."

His curiosity grew because whatever she had to
tell him, she was worried about it.

She sat on the edge of a sofa and he sat facing her
in a wingback chair. Her hands were locked together
in her lap and her knuckles were white. Startled, he
reached over and placed his hand on hers. Her hands
felt like ice and he looked up to meet an even more
worried gaze.

"What the hell, Camilla? What's wrong?" He
thought about his dad's heart trouble and a cold fear
gripped him.

"Noah, I've just had so much difficulty with our
breakup. I can't deal with your male ways sometimes.
You know you take charge. I don't want to spend
weekends on your ranch. I don't even really like country music. We're not compatible."

"I've got all that, Camilla. We've been over it,"
he said, watching her wring her hands, which he'd
never seen her do before. He leaned close and covered her hands with his. "Camilla, are you ill?" he
asked gently.

"Oh, no. No, it's not that," she said, sounding startled. He waited while silence stretched between them. He couldn't imagine what was wrong.

"Camilla, just tell me," he coaxed softly.

"This morning I started to call you a dozen times and cancel seeing you today. I don't want to do this."

"You're not sick, but you have to tell me something unpleasant that you don't want to tell me. Is that what's going on?" She bit her lip and stared at him. "Something is worrying you and in some manner it involves me or you wouldn't be telling me all this. What the hell is wrong? Just say it and let's go from there."

She took a deep breath. "I've done something I should not have done and Thane knew it."

Noah frowned because he had no clue what she was talking about, but at least she didn't have a dreaded disease and he was relieved for that. He removed his hands from hers and thought about the letter from Thane. "What on earth has your brother asked you to do? And it involves me. He was trying to get us back together just like he got Mike and Vivian together, wasn't he? You don't need to get so totally undone over that. I can't imagine anything you've done that you shouldn't have unless he's given you a guilty conscience over breaking it off with me. Is that it?"

"Absolutely not," she said, shocking him.

"Then what the hell could possibly be this bad that Thane knew and that affects me?"

"I haven't told you something I should have told

you, so just get ready for a shock." She reached over beside her on a table and picked up a framed picture that had been facedown. He'd noticed it but had given it little thought. "Here's Ethan's picture. Noah, please forgive me and try to understand."

He took the picture, and as he looked down at it, he felt his heart clutch.

Six

Noah

As he stared at the face of the boy in the photo, he remembered how Thane, when he had been wounded and barely conscious, suddenly had looked at Noah with clarity and determination and told him in a strong voice to put his nephew's present in the baby's hand. Thane had been determined that Noah see Thane's nephew. Just as determined as Camilla had been to keep him from seeing the child. Speechless, he looked at the picture again and knew he was looking at his own child.

His eyes met Camilla's. Tears spilled over and ran down her cheeks.

"I got you pregnant when I was home on furlough

before you married?" he asked, knowing that was the only time it could have been.

Nodding, she closed her eyes. "Yes."

Still stunned, he could feel his heart pound. "Why didn't you tell me?" he couldn't keep from asking. "Oh, dammit, Camilla." He looked at the picture, at the baby with black curls and blue eyes, and he felt as if he held his own baby picture.

"He has to be over a year old now."

"He's fifteen months," she said without looking at him. She had a handkerchief over her eyes as she cried. "Noah, I'm sorry. When I had him, you were overseas."

"Have you heard of a father's rights?" he asked, and he couldn't keep the anger out of his voice.

"I know I did something wrong, but we weren't getting along."

"This never once occurred to me."

"It hasn't to most people."

"But Thane… When did he see Ethan? Thane wasn't home after Ethan was born."

She shook her head. "Thane hounded me to send a picture. I didn't send it until I got him to promise he would keep what I wrote to himself. Thane always kept his word. I wrote Thane the truth and that I hadn't told you and I sent him a little picture. Of course, he urged me to let you know."

"I can't believe you kept this from me and my family." Noah stood and walked away from her, taking the picture with him to look at it while fury rocked him. "Anyone who sees this baby would know he's my child. I can dredge up baby pictures that look just like this."

"I know." Tears still ran down her cheeks and she wiped her eyes.

Noah thought about all the time she had known that he was a dad.

"We need to work out what we're going to do," she said.

"Oh, yeah. Camilla, I want my son."

She lowered the handkerchief to look at him, standing and facing him. "Noah, I'm sorry you didn't know sooner. It wouldn't have brought you home any quicker. Please forgive me."

"It wouldn't have brought me home sooner, but my family would have known they had a grandchild."

"You can tell them today and I can take him to see them this week."

"Dammit," he said, fury making him hot as he stared at her. "I'll take him to see them. But that's not the point, Camilla. It's time. Time matters. For fifteen months—for almost twenty-four months, counting your pregnancy—my parents could have looked forward to and enjoyed knowing their grandson before I came home."

"They can now, Noah."

He walked closer to her. "Camilla, while I was gone, my dad had two heart attacks and heart surgery. Time does matter and you cost them months of happiness," he said, his words cold and bitter.

All color drained from her face. "Oh, Noah, I'm so sorry," she said, putting her hand up as if to reach to touch him, while tears poured down her cheeks. But she put her hand down and looked away. "I didn't know and I never thought of something like that. Did Thane know about your dad?"

"No. Ben just told me when I got home."

"That's dreadful and what I did is dreadful. I didn't know about your dad. I'm so sorry. I've made some big mistakes. Is your dad's health why you haven't gone to the ranch?"

"Yes. I'm staying in Dallas for a while so I can be with my parents."

As he thought about what he wanted to do, he faced Camilla. "I want my parents to know Ethan. I want Ethan with me half the time." Color drained from her face. Even so, she raised her chin.

"I've been thinking about it. We'll have to work out how we'll share him, but for right now, since you don't know him or how to take care of him, move in with me. I've got a big home and it's already arranged for a baby. I know moving to my house will put a temporary crimp in your social life, but for a little while, move in and let Ethan get used to you and get to know him. That way, I'll be here for him, because he needs me, Noah."

As he thought it over, anger still burned in him, but she made sense and his son needed his mother. "You're probably right. I can do that."

"I'll give you a tour when we can. I have a big studio here and I paint early in the mornings, but we can adjust that. There's plenty of room.

"I need to fly to Chicago next week to arrange my art show. It'll leave you two here together. My mom will keep him in a pinch, so take him to her when you need to go out. I have two nannies I use and I'll leave their names. Once you introduce him to your family, I imagine your parents will want him sometimes, too."

"Yes, they will. Right now the only symptom Dad seems to have is he's more tired, so my mom can take care of Ethan and I'm sure she'll want to. Ben and Hallie will probably want some time with him. They've tried to get pregnant and haven't been able to. This will take some pressure off them and that may help because the doctor said they were physically able to have a baby."

He ran a hand through his hair. "Dammit, Camilla, family is the most important thing in life. My family means the world to me and I want a family of my own, but I also never wanted to rush into a relationship and marry until I knew damn well the woman was the right person for me. Right now, marriage isn't a solution for us at all and I'm sure you agree."

"Yes, I do, Noah. We have big problems between us."

"This hurts," he said. Camilla stepped close to him to put her hands on his shoulders. His heart drummed, and in spite of his shock and anger, he still wanted to put his arms around her.

"Noah, I made the wrong choices. I've hurt you

and your family and I'm truly sorry. I hope it isn't too late to make up for that."

He was torn between desire and anger. Right now, he was aware of her hands on his shoulders, of her enticing perfume, of her big hazel eyes with long brown lashes. His gaze lowered to her full lips and his pulse pounded. She always smelled sweet and her softness was irresistible. He fought the urge to wrap his arms around her and kiss her, and he simply nodded. "All right, Camilla. We'll go from here."

She dropped her hands and stepped away, but turned back. "If you want a DNA test, we can do that. I promise you, this is your baby, but if you would like a DNA test, I'll get one for you."

He shook his head and held up the picture she had handed to him. "This is like looking at my own baby picture. I don't need a DNA test."

"That's what Thane wrote after I sent him Ethan's picture. He didn't know you when you were a baby, but he must have seen pictures of you. Ethan has your black curly hair and your blue eyes. You'll see."

He heard a baby cry on a monitor.

"There he is, right on cue," she said. "I'll go get him."

She left and Noah looked at the picture again. He was a dad—no nine months to get ready for that news. His anger was fading and he was beginning to think about the immediate future. He would move in with Camilla. That made the most sense. He couldn't imagine how they could live under the same roof without giving in to sex, which would only lead to an even bigger emotional risk. But she was right. He needed to learn how to take care of his baby, and he couldn't take his child away from his mother and put him with strangers.

He was going to have his son in his life and he just hoped he didn't have to fight Camilla in court about it. He wanted equal time, joint custody, whatever it took. He thought about Mia. He'd liked going out with her the couple of times they'd dated, when he'd thought Camilla was out of his life, but that had all changed this past hour. Seeing Mia would have to be put on hold. Right now he needed to get to know his son and he needed to be able to deal with Camilla on some level because they would have to both be involved in their child's life.

He heard her talking before she entered the room and then she came through the doorway with a baby in her arms. He felt as if a giant hand squeezed his heart and all his anger evaporated. He couldn't take his gaze off the baby, who was wearing little jeans, socks and a red T-shirt. He had black curly hair as tangled as Noah's had been as far back as he could remember. The baby had rosy cheeks and big blue eyes. He held a little brown stuffed bear in one arm and kept his gaze on Noah, seeming to be as curious about Noah as Noah was about him.

Noah's heart pounded and he felt overwhelmed. She walked close, stopping in front of him, and Noah could smell baby powder. "Here's your son, Noah," she said softly. "This is Ethan. It's officially Ethan Warner. By the time Ethan was born, Aiden and I had officially been divorced for months and there was no reason to take his name. Aiden knew the truth, that this was not his child, and he left Texas and said he wasn't coming back. Everyone who knew me didn't question that I named him Ethan Warner because Aiden was long out of my life." She smiled at her baby and then looked at Noah. "Do you want to hold him?"

Emotions ran through Noah: joy, gratitude, curiosity, amazement and uncertainty. "I don't know one little thing about babies even though all my siblings are younger than I am." He looked at Camilla. "Will he be scared?"

"I don't think so," she said and placed the baby in Noah's arms. Ethan was warm, smelled of baby powder and was astonishing to Noah.

"My son," he said in amazement. He looked at Camilla. "You should have let me know. I might have been able to get home for the birth. How long were you in labor?"

"Not long. He weighed eight pounds and one ounce."

"I think he's a fine-looking baby."

She smiled. "I think so, too."

"Our baby. That just isn't real yet. You went all through that pregnancy without me. Did you have morning sickness?"

"No. Everything about my pregnancy was easy except the daddy part, and that was my own doing."

Noah looked at Ethan. "Hi, Ethan," he said, and Ethan smiled, reaching tiny fingers to touch Noah's beard.

Camilla placed her hand on Noah's shoulder. "Daddy," she said clearly. Then she looked at Noah. "Ethan's a man of few words, so don't expect much in the way of conversation."

Noah laughed. "I think he's fascinating." His smile faded and he looked intently at her. "This baby is going to bless my whole family. In a minute I'll call them. I know they'll be home tonight. Can I take Ethan to meet them?"

"Noah, he's your baby, too. Of course you can," she said.

"Can he stay overnight with them soon?"

"Of course. You don't need my permission for those things because you're his dad."

"I'm on a roll. Maybe I should ask if I can take him to the ranch."

She drew a deep breath and he smiled.

"I'm teasing you right now. The day will come when I will want to take him to the ranch, but not now." He looked at Ethan again. "He's marvelous. Ethan, you're a first-class baby," he said. "Does he sleep through the night?"

"Nearly always. He's been an easy baby. And a happy baby."

"That is really good news," he said, turning to look at her again. She gazed back with a worried frown and he turned to his baby. "I'm a dad. That is the most wonderful news."

"I didn't know you'd be this happy about it."

"I'm in awe. I'm thrilled. I need some dad lessons. I don't know how to take care of him."

"That's why I suggested you move in here. I can show you how."

Noah couldn't seem to take his eyes off the child. "Ethan, I'm your daddy."

"Daddy, Ethan," she repeated and placed her hand on Noah's shoulder again. Ethan held one arm out to reach for Camilla, so Noah handed her their son.

"I think he's had enough of me."

Camilla took him. "You did well for the first time and he liked you."

"I'm glad you know his signals. All he did was stare and smile. I'm going to call my folks and tell them I want to come by and talk to them, that I have a surprise. Then I'll come back and get you and Ethan and take you over. We're not going to just walk in the door with him and announce that I have a son."

"Just go and talk to them, and when you're ready, call and I can drive to your folks' house. You don't have to come back to get us."

"I'll come get you because it will give them a chance to get used to this idea of being grandparents. Stefanie is going to love this." He turned to look at Camilla, who stood only inches away, and she gazed up at him. Once again she had tears in her eyes.

"Why the tears now?"

"I've made a muddle of things and I'm so sorry, especially about your dad. That possibility never occurred to me. We still have big problems separating us. This baby needs both of us."

"Yeah, I know. I'll worry about that one tomorrow. Just take tonight and let's celebrate. He's still under your roof and he's with you and he's with me. My family will be thrilled beyond anything you can imagine. Frankly, I'm thrilled, Camilla. I didn't know I would feel this way about a baby, but I do."

He looked intently at her and slipped his hand behind her head.

"It wasn't my fault, but I'm sorry I wasn't there with you when he was born."

Her expression changed as her eyes widened and she looked surprised. "I'll admit, Noah, I had some rough moments because you weren't here. My brothers tried to make up for it, but Mason and Logan have busy lives and they're single. They were nice to try to be there for me. Logan lives in Dallas, so he was around often at first. Thanks to you for saying that now. And I'm sorry about your dad. If I had known…" Her voice trailed away.

Noah looked at Ethan. "This will make up for it in a lot of ways. You can't imagine how happy Ethan is going to make my family. It'll help us get through what's happening and what's to come." She looked up at him and Noah wanted to wrap his arms around her and Ethan, and he wanted to kiss away all the problems between them and take her to bed with him. Taking a deep breath, he turned away, because that wasn't going to happen and their problems would not go away.

"Oh, here's the package from your brother that I'm to put in Ethan's hands. I don't think I have to do that now. I get what he was after. He wanted me to know you and I have a son."

"Yes, he did. Thane was a wonderful big brother, but sometimes he meddled."

"Thank God he did this time," Noah said, giving her the package.

She turned it over in her hands. "I have this instead of my brother," she said. "I miss him."

"I know. He was a great guy." Noah pulled out his phone. "I'll head home now. I hate to leave. Let me get some quick pictures. Can I take this one now?" He held up the photo she'd shown him. "I'll give it back."

"Keep it, Noah," she said, smiling at him as he took the small framed picture of Ethan. He took some more pictures on his phone and she smiled. "Noah, stop. You'll have fifty pictures in another minute. We have loads and you'll take a bunch at your house."

He smiled and stepped to her. "I'll stop and I'll go see my folks. I know things aren't great between us, but for tonight, let's forget the differences and celebrate my discovery that I'm a dad."

"It won't solve a thing, but I'm willing to have a celebration tonight. Sort of a temporary truce, if there is such a thing."

"Goodbye, sweet baby," Noah said, leaning down to look Ethan straight in the eye. Noah laughed and straightened. "He is a man of few words. When do they start talking?"

"He should by now. It varies, but he's going to be one that's on the late side. He says some words. *Bye-bye*, *bear*, *mine*—he has a tiny vocabulary. It'll come, Noah."

"Well, I think he's marvelous. Maybe babies should wait and come when they are about twelve months old. They're more interesting."

"I don't think pregnant mothers would vote for that one," she said, smiling and shaking her head. "You've really surprised me once we got past the shock and anger, which I understood and expected. I didn't expect this enthusiasm and joy, but I'm so glad and so relieved."

"I've never really given a thought to being a dad. Well, I'll run," he said as he opened the front door. She followed him outside and stood on the top step of the wide front porch.

"Goodbye, Ethan, you adorable child. Ahh, Camilla, this is wonderful news. It'll complicate the hell out of your life and my life, but it'll be worth it. I'll call you after I talk to my parents," he said and went to his car in long strides, soon leaving down the long, sweeping drive and heading for his parents' home, happy that he was going to have great news for his whole family.

Stefanie, though, might have a moment or two because she was friends with Mia and hoped Mia would replace Camilla in his life. He'd had fun with Mia.

She was gorgeous, sexy, appealing, and she accepted him totally as he was without wanting him to transform his life and turn into a different kind of man. For right now, though, he wanted to get to know his son. That came first.

And if the time came when Camilla was part of the bargain, he'd deal with it the best he could.

Camilla

Camilla went inside and closed the door, looking down at Ethan. "Now you've met your daddy and surprise, surprise—he loves you a whole, whole lot. Surprised me because I never expected that reaction." She thought about Noah's dad and hurt for Noah. She was sorry about his dad's heart trouble, but medical science could do wonders. "Tonight is great, but tomorrow, your daddy and I will have to start making decisions and it's going to be, oh, so tough," she told Ethan, who chewed on his bear.

"In the meantime, let's get out your best outfit so you look your cutest to meet your grandparents. You'll meet your paternal grandparents tonight and maybe aunts and uncles. They won't be able to resist you and your charming ways, especially since you had the good sense to look like your dad," Camilla said as she took Ethan to her room to bathe him in her bathroom. She'd picked up Thane's package before she'd left the living room and now she placed it on her dresser before taking Ethan to bathe him. She would open Thane's little package afterward.

Later, after bathing Ethan, she put him on the floor, where he could play with his toys while she got ready. First, she picked up the package from Thane and sat on the floor with Ethan to carefully open it, once again feeling a tie to her brother. When she unwrapped the brown paper, she held a child's book of nursery rhymes. She opened it. Thane had written:

> To Ethan:
> I hope your parents read these verses to you and you like them as much as I did. I wish I could watch you grow up. Hug your mommy and your daddy for me. I love all of you.
> Much love to my nephew from Uncle Thane

Camilla hurt and missed her brother. What a sacrifice soldiers made to give up their lives. Wiping away tears, she couldn't be annoyed with him for making sure that Noah learned that he had a son. She should have let him know when she was pregnant or shortly after she gave birth to Ethan. She never expected him to be so thrilled and happy over becoming a dad.

She put the wrappings and the book back on her dresser and her thoughts shifted to Noah again and how happy he had been over Ethan. Never once had she expected Noah to be so delighted to discover he was a father. She knew a tough time lay ahead. He'd made that clear tonight. For the rest of her life she would remember tonight when he said, *I want my son*. That was the downside. He would fight to have Ethan equally. Her family was wealthy, but Noah was wealthier, even without his family's fortune. He could certainly afford the fight.

He said to take things a day at a time and that was what she would do tonight. Tonight should be filled with joy for Noah and his family.

And what about later tonight?

She suspected he would stay tonight in a guest bedroom in her house. If they started sleeping together, she would just have a far bigger hurt when he moved out. She had to guard her heart because when he was happy, Noah could be incredibly charming.

But could she keep her distance, not only resist him, but keep her hands off him?

Noah

As he drove, Noah smiled. He called Ben's secretary and asked her to do a big favor and call Ben's best florist to order a huge bouquet of flowers sent ASAP and to put it on Noah's bill. He gave her Camilla's name and address. He asked them to put a small stuffed toy in it, if possible. Ben's secretary knew Noah and she laughed and said she would.

He was a dad and he had an adorable baby who looked just like him. This would be such good news for his parents. He wasn't going to think about what could have been or what should have been. They would learn about Ethan now and go from there, and from tonight on, it would be fun and exciting to have a baby in the family.

Once again he thought about Mia. Tomorrow he would call her and tell her about his son. She might not be thrilled to learn he was a dad.

Problems lay ahead with Camilla, too. They hadn't solved anything. They had probably complicated their lives and they might be headed for a huge court battle over rights.

Within minutes he turned into the familiar big circle drive and parked in front of his parents' two-story Tudor mansion that had an east wing and a six-car garage with an apartment over it. Ben's car was in the wide drive with Stefanie's red sports car parked behind it. Eli's car wasn't there, but he worked later and lived farther away. Noah had told Ben to round everyone up, that he wanted to talk to all of them and that he had a surprise. Noah had ordered a big rib dinner to be delivered to the house and he caught the enticing scent when he stepped onto the porch.

Excitement gripped him and he knew he would remember this day for the rest of his life. He wanted to laugh and shout for joy. In the coming days he intended to focus on his baby. He and Camilla hadn't settled one little thing and now the stakes would be infinitely higher with their baby in the middle.

Their baby... How good that sounded. He refused to consider any if-onlys. He crossed the porch and entered, hearing voices and laughter in the big living room.

"Hey, I'm here," he called, entering the living room and greeting them individually as he moved around the room.

Ben turned and smiled. "Okay, he's here and he's got a surprise for us and a big grin, so it's a good surprise. Let's hear it and then I'll go get you something to drink. Get us out of this suspense. You look as if you just found a gold mine in your yard."

His dad was still seated, not coming to his feet as he had always done when someone entered, and Noah hoped he was feeling reasonably well. His mother entered with a tray of crackers and healthy fruit and veggie snacks that she put on a table.

"Well, what is this big surprise you have?" she asked him. "And don't tell me you got us all together to hear about a new bull or new horse."

"Oh, it's better than a new horse," he said. They all gazed at him, waiting, Ben with his arm casually across Hallie's shoulders, Stefanie's eyes sparkling.

"I'm not sure where to start," he said as he looked around the room. "Camilla and I— Well, you know we had stopped seeing each other when I left for the service. But when I came back for a furlough about two years ago…" He noticed the minute he said Camilla's name, Stefanie's sparkle vanished and was replaced by a frown.

He started again. "Camilla had some news for me—a big surprise. I'll bring her over this evening, but I wanted to tell you first." He crossed the room to his mother to put his arm around her. "Mom and Dad, all my family, I'm so happy and I hope you are, too. I'm the father of a fifteen-month-old boy, Ethan."

His mother hugged him while Hallie shrieked with joy and rushed to hug him next. His dad stood to shake his hand and then Ben clapped him on the back. He glanced across the room and saw Stefanie with a deep frown as she stared at him. He smiled at her and turned to his mother.

"You're bringing them over for us to see your baby tonight?"

"Yes, I am. I think he's adorable."

"Noah, Camilla has let everyone think her baby was fathered by the man she married and divorced," Stefanie said.

"Yes, she didn't correct anyone about it. I'm sure some people knew, but none of us. Thane knew the truth and wrote her, urging her to tell me and all of us, so she has."

Ben shook his hand while he grinned. "I'm so happy for you. You can't imagine. This is a blessing for all of us."

His dad put his arm across Noah's shoulders. "That's the best news I've had in a long time, son. You'll be a fine dad."

"If I am, it's because of you," Noah said, hugging his dad.

"Hey, bro, I just got here. What's this about you being a dad?" Eli, Noah's youngest brother, asked, crossing the room to shake Noah's hand. Noah looked into another pair of eyes as blue as his own. Eli's black hair had a slight wave like Ben's.

"That's right, Eli," Noah said. "Camilla and I have a fifteen-month-old boy, Ethan Warner."

"Congratulations! Fantastic, man! Wedding bells will come next, eh?"

"Don't go so fast. I'm just trying to adjust to my new status as a dad."

"When do we get to meet the little guy?"

"As soon as I go get them. I wanted to come tell you first before I walk into the house with him."

"Noah, go get your baby for us to see," his mother said.

"I'll get the drinks," Ben said. "What do you want, Eli? Your usual vodka?"

"You got it, but stay here and I'll get the drinks." Eli left for the bar with their mother going along talking to him. Noah turned to face Stefanie.

"Noah, don't you want a DNA test before you announce you're the dad? Camilla might be saying this to get you back."

He laughed. "Stef, I don't need a DNA test. This is my baby."

"You don't know that for certain," she said.

"She might be right," Ben replied.

"I'm the oldest, so none of you remember me as a baby, but you've seen plenty of my baby pictures. How's this?" He went to the entryway to a table where he had placed the framed picture facedown when he had arrived. Carrying it, he returned to the family room to his sister and Ben, who had moved closer. "Here's my baby, little Ethan."

"Noah——" Stefanie started to say as she took the picture and looked at it. Frowning, she raised her head. "You have a baby picture just like this. Have you seen this baby?"

"Yes, I have. That's his picture, but it looks like one of mine."

"Sure as hell does," Ben added, peering over at the photo. "I've seen your baby pictures and they're interchangeable with this one." He walked away to get his drink.

Stefanie let out a long breath and shook her head. "He's your baby," she said, sounding shocked. "I didn't think this would really be your baby, but it is. There is no denying it—he looks like every one of us in this room."

"Stef, don't sound as if the world just ended. This is great news for our folks, and it's good news for Ben and Hallie because it takes the pressure off them," he said, speaking softly and talking fast. "Stop match-making for me. And tonight, enjoy your new nephew. You're Aunt Stefanie now."

"Oh, my, I'm an aunt." She looked up at Noah and smiled. "I'm sorry about you and Camilla, but this is wonderful. This is good for Mom and Dad. I'm sorry, Noah. I want you to be happy and you seemed happier with Mia than you've been with Camilla, but this is your baby. Mercy, he looks just like you."

"He certainly does look like me. He's got my wonderful disposition, too," he said and smiled. Laughing, Stefanie still stared at the picture. Noah patted her shoulder. "Lighten up, Stef. This is good news. You're going to like being an aunt and he is one happy baby."

She looked up, sighed and then nodded. "Sorry, Noah. I just worry about you and I think Camilla is going to hurt you."

"Let me worry about that. Enjoy my son."

"My, oh, my. Your son. I can't believe it."

"C'mon—we'll show Mom and Dad his picture. I have some pictures I took with my phone, too. In just a few minutes, I'll go get Camilla and Ethan."

"Have you told Mia?"

"Not yet. I just found out and I wanted the family to be the first to know. I'll call her tomorrow. Stefanie, Mia and I have a good time, but there's nothing serious between us. Stop matchmaking. And speaking of—who are you going out with?"

"Don't start in on me. As far as Mia is concerned, I just want you to be happy and you haven't been."

"I've been overseas fighting and going through losing Thane and some other buddies. Things will straighten out with time," he said, wondering if and how they really would. His life had just gotten a lot more complicated.

"Okay. Go get this little baby of yours. I can't believe I'm an aunt. Aunt Stefanie." She laughed. "I want to meet my nephew. I hope I like him."

"I think you will. Pretend he's me."

Smiling, she shook her head. "Go get this baby for us to see before Dad gets too tired to enjoy the moment."

"You're right. I'm gone. You can show the picture around."

"You realize you just tied your life to Camilla's for a long time."

"Yeah, I know." He turned and left to get his baby. His baby—he was still in shock. On the way he made a stop to buy champagne.

When Camilla opened the door, he drew a deep breath. She had changed into tan linen slacks and a matching linen blouse and she looked gorgeous. He looked into her wide hazel eyes and his heart beat faster as desire filled the look he received in return.

"Come in," she said, and her voice was breathless. When her gaze went to his mouth, he fought an inner battle because he wanted to take her into his arms and kiss her. Trying to control his desire, he stepped inside and walked past her. As a faint whiff of her perfume teased him, he fought the urge to look around at her. How was he going to live in the same house with her and keep from carrying her off to bed?

Seven

Camilla

Camilla's heartbeat jumped to a faster pace. Noah stood facing her and he was so good-looking, he took her breath away. Her heart pounded, and desire, the longing to take two steps and put her arms around him, was intense. In spite of all the problems, she wanted to walk into his arms and kiss him. But she knew that was impossible, would only create bigger problems. Trying to bank her longing, she smiled at him. "We're ready to go. I have Ethan's things. But first I have to ask—was your family happy?"

"They are overjoyed and can't wait to see him. You look gorgeous," he said, making her heart beat faster when she looked into his eyes and saw the desire that filled his expression.

"Thanks." She looked at Ethan in her arms in a navy jumper and white shirt. "How does he look to you?"

"Perfect. Hi, Ethan," Noah said, leaning a little closer. She could detect Noah's aftershave and that made her think of kissing him. She looked at her baby in her arms and tried to stop thinking about Noah.

Ethan smiled and held out his arm.

"Hey, he wants me to take him. You think?" Noah's dark brows arched in surprise.

"Don't sound so shocked. Maybe he senses something. Let me get his things. He never travels lightly. We'll go in my car because of the baby seat."

"Okay. I'll take Ethan and you put this in your fridge." He handed her a bottle of champagne. She'd been so intent on looking at Noah that she hadn't noticed it till now. "We'll celebrate when we come home. When you're ready, we'll go," he said, taking Ethan from her.

Noah's warm hands brushing hers and just that slight contact sizzled. She was grateful for the champagne that she had to refrigerate.

When she returned to the living room moments later, Noah turned to her. "I'll drive if you want."

"Sure," she said, giving him the keys with another brush of hands. They looked at each other at the same time and she realized he had felt something too from the casual brush of hands.

"Why do we do that to each other?" she asked.

"Who can explain attraction? We're as different as fire and ice."

"Well, I'm rather happy for some of those differences," she said, knowing she shouldn't flirt with him or encourage the attraction.

Noah must have known it too, because he held his ground. "We're complicating our lives from the first moment. But somehow—"

"Let's go," she said, not wanting to play with the fire that was burning between them.

She turned on the house alarm and followed him out to the car.

When they arrived at the front door to his parents' house, she handed Ethan to Noah. "You take him in and show him around."

The minute they entered the living room, everyone huddled around Ethan. Noah handed him to his mother, who turned to take him to his dad. Noah stepped back beside Camilla. One glance at him and she guessed that he was thinking about losing his dad. Impulsively, she took Noah's warm hand.

When he turned and focused on her, she dropped his hand. "Sorry. I just thought you were worrying."

"I was. It's a bittersweet moment."

Noah glanced down at Camilla and laced his fingers through hers, holding her hand and stepping a fraction closer, making her think about going home with him and making love, something she wanted more each time she was with him even though she knew she needed to keep her distance. Working out how they would share Ethan could pose monumental problems on top of the ones they already had.

"Go join them, Noah. I'll take some pictures." Noah crossed the room and stood close to his parents while they held Ethan. She looked at all the black-haired, blue-eyed Grants. Ethan fit right in and looked like one of the family. Only Noah's mom had blue-green eyes and red hair with white strands now. His dad still had some black in his hair, but it was mostly gray, making her think that was the way Noah would look someday. She realized this would probably be the only time she would be included in a Grant family gathering. She and Noah were no longer a couple and he would be taking Ethan alone to see his family. That realization hurt, yet every time she questioned her feelings about Noah being a rancher and another alpha male, she came back to the same decision—that wasn't what she wanted in her life. But moments like this still hurt.

Stefanie glanced her way and then crossed the room to her. "We didn't mean to leave you out. Everyone is so excited over Ethan. I can't believe I'm an aunt. He is precious."

"Thanks, Stefanie. Go back and join the family. Ethan is new to all of you. I've had a lot of time to look at him. I don't mind."

"Why don't you join us?" she replied. But before she turned to go back, she said, "I'm surprised how happy he is, and he's not scared of all these new people passing him around and looking at him."

Camilla smiled. "Maybe because all of you look just like he does, he feels comfortable."

Stefanie laughed. "If you're okay, I'm going back. I don't know beans about a baby, but this is fun and wonderful for my folks."

"I'm glad," Camilla said, keeping her smile, but she hurt because she wasn't part of the family and she wouldn't ever be.

Noah

While Noah talked to his siblings, he watched Camilla, who sat with his parents, helping them with Ethan if they needed it. His gaze slid over her and his heart beat faster. She looked radiant tonight, laughing and smiling with his family, happy with her little boy. Even though he knew he couldn't, he wanted to take her home to bed, to hold her and make love to her, to shower her with gratitude for this baby. As she talked to his folks, she shook her head and her hair swung away from her face and Noah could remember how it spread over his bare shoulder when they were in bed together, an image he needed to get out of his thoughts now.

The family and Ethan seemed to have a fun time and finally Ethan slept in Noah's dad's arms while his mother was beside them, looking at Ethan every few minutes. When Camilla glanced at Noah, he suspected she was ready to go home because the hour was getting late.

"It's a weeknight and we should go now," Noah said as he stood.

As he expected, it was another thirty minutes before they were in her car with Noah driving and Ethan asleep in his car seat. They spoke about how happy his family was, how eager to hold Ethan. But all Noah could concentrate on was Camilla. She was three feet away in her seat, yet he could feel her.

At her house he helped her put Ethan to bed and finally stood beside her over Ethan's crib. Noah draped his arm casually across her shoulders as he stood looking down at Ethan.

"He's a marvel to me. I wish I'd been here when he was born."

"We can't undo that now."

They walked out of the room together and he still had his arm across her shoulders. "My room adjoins his," she said. "I can put you in an adjoining room on the other side, or there's a big suite across the hall."

"Give me the suite and I can spread out, unless that's an inconvenience. You have a big house for one person and now a baby."

"I have a big art studio downstairs and I wanted lots of room for Ethan. My family is here sometimes, too." She shrugged. "It is big, but I like it. I have someone who comes to clean it. Someone to take care of the yard. And I have a nanny who's here when I need her. And a backup nanny. But Ethan is easy, so

I take care of him most of the time myself. My folks really aren't into babysitting, but they keep him occasionally."

"Sounds like you have things worked out. Let's go open the champagne and celebrate my fatherhood."

She stiffened and for a moment he thought she would decline. Perhaps because she too thought that champagne and celebration could lead to kisses and bed? Just the thought made his heart beat faster.

"By all means," she finally said. "I didn't know how you'd take the news, but you've been great and I think you're going to be a wonderful dad."

"I hope so. I had a good model."

Camilla

The lights were low in her big family room, giving a cozy atmosphere that couldn't quiet Camilla's nerves as she watched Noah open the champagne and pour the bubbling liquid, half filling two flutes. He had rolled up his sleeves and unfastened the top buttons of his blue shirt. His thick curls were a tangle and some fell on his forehead. In the low light he looked strong, handsome and sexy, and she felt she was headed for disaster if she didn't walk away in the next few minutes. She couldn't leave, though. She had spent too many nights missing him, wanting him with her. Knowing better, she still couldn't resist this small celebration with him. He was home safe from fighting and he had been great with Ethan.

Ethan was happy with Noah and with his whole family and that was definitely a cause for celebration. She knew problems were ahead because she and Noah had different outlooks on life and they both were strong-willed people.

He picked up one flute to hand to her and then took the other for himself. He turned to her and held up his glass. "Here's to you, Camilla, for giving me our son. He is already a joy for me and my family."

Noah's voice was husky, his blue eyes dark with desire, and she felt headed for catastrophe as she clinked her flute lightly against his and sipped her champagne. She remembered how she had wanted Noah at her side when Ethan was born. She wanted Noah's strong arms around her now. She wanted his kisses, his loving, even though a night of kisses and hot sex would just make life more difficult.

"I'm still shocked how happy you are about Ethan."

"Of course I'm happy about him. Family is everything, and you saw what a joy he was to my family." He gazed at her and set his drink on a table, turning to take hers from her hand and put it beside his. Her heart drummed and she knew she should stop him, but she couldn't say anything. She ached to kiss and hold him and find the paradise they once knew when they were together.

"Noah, this is just going to complicate our lives all over again," she whispered while her heart pounded. She gazed up at his thickly lashed eyes that made her pulse race.

"Darlin', we complicated the hell out of our lives when I got you pregnant. There's no going back on that one. I know we've got bad times ahead of us, but tonight let's really celebrate. We're Ethan's mom and dad, and tonight let's rejoice in that and in each other. We can go back to the fight tomorrow or next week or whenever. I know we will go back to it because it goes deep and isn't something that has an easy fix. Just one night's celebration."

His seductive request was too tempting, but she knew she would have monumental regrets because she wasn't getting over him. And he was right—the problems weren't going away. Noah would always be an alpha male, always be a rancher. No matter how big a folly tonight might be, she couldn't resist. He was looking at her now as if she were the only woman on earth and as necessary to him as breathing.

"Noah, we're going to have giant regrets, but I can't say no to you when you're so overjoyed about our parenthood. Ethan is a constant joy. You'll love him so much and your family will, too. I guess we'll just sink into more difficulties and go ahead and celebrate tonight. Just tonight. It was a lonely childbirth in spite of my family. You weren't here and didn't know and neither was Thane. Frankly, Logan and my mom finally came to the hospital just before he was born, but I didn't know they were there until quite a while after he was born. Mason sent a huge bouquet and came the next week. I'd like to celebrate tonight because I couldn't when he was born."

Noah slid his arm around her waist and she felt the solid muscle. He pulled her up tight against him and her heart pounded.

"Tonight, I want to forget everything except becoming a dad. I want you, Camilla."

"Ah, Noah, we shouldn't—" She couldn't keep from saying the words, even though she had already decided she would celebrate with him tonight and she had known that that meant making love.

"Oh, yeah, we should, and you want to. Oh, baby, do you ever want to. It shows in your eyes." He tilted her chin up and looked at her intently. "Tell me you don't want me to kiss you."

"Noah—" She hurt and she should tell him, but she wanted to kiss him with all her being.

"That's what I thought. You want to kiss as badly as I do." He bent his head and his lips covered hers and she opened her mouth to kiss him in return, wanting his kiss with all her heart. His arm tightened around her and he leaned over her. She wrapped her arms around his neck to cling to him as she kissed him, her tongue sliding over his, his tongue stroking hers and her mouth.

She moaned with pleasure while her heart pounded and she thrust her hips against him. He was hard, wonderful, holding her easily with one arm while his other hand ran lightly over her curves, caressing her.

She slipped her hand between them to unbutton his shirt completely and then slide her hand over his bare chest, tangling her fingers in the curly black hair.

"Ah, darlin', how many long, empty nights I've dreamed of holding you, touching you and kissing you."

His words were seductive, his hands magic on her, his mouth setting her ablaze with longing. "Noah, you'll never know how much I've missed you and wanted you," she whispered, turning her head and then running her tongue over the curve of his ear while she ran her hand along his thigh.

"I want to touch and kiss you all night long. You were my dream, my wish, my longing while I was gone," Noah said between kisses as he unbuttoned her blouse and pushed it away. When he slipped his hand beneath her bra and cupped her breast, she gasped as he caressed her.

"You're so soft. There were too many lonely nights, too much violence, too much fighting and too much dying. This is life and love and hope. I can't tell you how many nights I've dreamed of you and wanted you in my arms. You've given me the greatest gift possible. I want you, Camilla," he whispered, peeling away her bra and slacks. He held her, his gaze roaming over her.

"Beautiful," he said in a hoarse voice.

"Noah, we're just going to make things worse," she whispered, but she didn't really care. She had already made her decision to make love to him, to stay in his arms all night long.

"Tonight that is absolutely impossible," he whispered and kissed away her protest. She was lost to the

moment, wanting him. It had been two years since
she had been in his arms and they had made love.
She suddenly wriggled free and pushed against him,
unfastening his belt, her hands shaking with haste as
she continued to peel away his clothes. She paused
while he yanked off his boots.

"I have to kiss you, Noah," she whispered. "You
just take my breath away and I want to kiss you. I
have to touch you," she repeated, trailing her hands on
his thighs, following her fingers with her mouth and
tongue, taking his thick rod in her hand and kissing
him, stroking him, running her other hand so lightly
between his legs and over his thighs.

He inhaled deeply, winding his fingers in her hair,
tangling it. He picked her up to place her on the bed,
moving on top of her. His eyes blazed with passion
as he gazed down at her, but his hand was incredibly
gentle when he brushed long strands of hair from
her face.

"You're beautiful. You're sexy and I want you. I
want to kiss and touch every inch of you and make
you want me and want to make love all night long.
I need you and we're just getting started." He bent
his head to kiss her belly while his hands were all
over her, caressing her breasts, her nipples, her inner
thighs as she writhed and moaned with pleasure as
much as need.

He trailed his tongue over her belly, up over first
one soft breast and then the other, stroking lightly,

slowly circling her nipples while his hands played over her.

"Noah…" She gasped. "Come love me," she said, tugging on his arms. He rolled her over on her stomach.

"Shh, let me kiss you. I've dreamed of you, your gorgeous body, your softness, your fiery sexiness." He trailed kisses along the backs of her thighs. Her hands knotted the sheet as she wriggled and let him kiss and touch her.

"Oh, Noah," she gasped, lost in sensation, wanting to kiss him, wanting him inside her, wanting his hardness, his hands all over her, her mouth on him.

He sat up once, pulling her up to face him. He wrapped his arm around her waist, leaning forward to kiss her. He raised his head to look at her again and she gazed into blue eyes that had darkened with passion.

Noah rolled on his side, taking her with him and gazing at her before pulling her close and kissing her, a kiss that made her want him desperately.

"You had my baby. Ah, darlin', we have a beautiful, wonderful son and my family already loves him and for that I will always be grateful to you. I want to make love to you, feel and caress and kiss you all night long. I want to find what really excites you."

"You have, Noah. Just holding me and kissing me." She turned his face to her and gazed into his eyes before leaning close to kiss him, running her tongue so slowly over his lips first.

He made a growling sound deep in his throat while his hand went to the back of her head to pull her forward and his tongue went deep into her mouth as he kissed her hard in return. Featherlight, his fingers caressed her breasts, and then he shifted to his side. His leg slid between hers, keeping hers apart while his hands moved over her intimately, rubbing and caressing her.

"Noah, I want to kiss you," she whispered, shifting to push him down. She moved over him, leaning close to run her tongue over his belly and his manhood, taking him in her hand to stroke and excite him as he had her.

"I want your mouth and hands all over me," she whispered. "I want mine all over you. I've dreamed of making love to you, dreamed of you being here with me."

Sitting up, he pulled her into his arms to kiss her passionately again, a kiss that made her heart pound and made her feel that, for the moment, he loved her with all his being. A kiss that made her feel as if they were the only two people in the world and they would always have each other. His mouth, hands and body, his thick manhood, mesmerized her.

While he held her tightly, she couldn't think beyond the moment or look at reality. Right now they kissed each other and that was enough.

He stepped off the bed to get a packet from his wallet.

"I'm on birth control," she said. He came back to

bed to place the condom beside the bed and stretch out beside her, drawing her into his embrace again.

"I think you told me that some twenty-four months ago."

"That was a fluke. It'll work this time."

"At the moment, I don't care. I can't change my plans at this point unless you absolutely want me to."

"I want you to kiss me."

"Anything to make the lady happy," he whispered, pulling her into his arms and kissing her.

She wrapped her arms around him, kissing him in return until he moved between her legs and paused to put on the condom. She watched him. He was hard, ready to love her, and the sight of him made her heart race. Noah was incredibly handsome, virile, so sexy. Tonight she couldn't, wouldn't, resist him. She would relish every moment of lovemaking and not think about tomorrow.

He lowered his weight and kissed her, entering her slowly as she wrapped her long legs around him and clung to him with her arms around his broad back that tapered to his narrow waist. She ran her hand over his hard bottom. He was all muscle, so incredibly appealing. She tightened her arms around him as he moved slowly, and she raised her hips to meet him, holding him close.

"Ah, Noah, I want you." She gasped, pleasure washing over her as he withdrew and plunged in again. She shifted higher, wanting him, moving beneath him until he began to thrust faster, and she moaned softly, holding him tightly, feeling the pressure coil inside as it built, until her climax burst and she cried out in pleasure.

"Noah." She sighed and thrust with him as he reached his climax and then sagged against her, turning to kiss her.

"Camilla, this was better than I dreamed of. I want you in my bed, in my arms all night."

"This time is okay, Noah. Tonight is a celebration of Ethan's birth and of you learning you're a dad. Tonight is special."

"Damn right it's special. In every way it's fantastic, being a dad, making love to you, holding your naked body against mine. This night is paradise on earth for me."

"It is for me, too," she whispered. "You can't imagine how sexy you are, how I want you and how marvelous this is."

"Yeah, for several hours," he said, and she heard a bitter note in his voice. She placed her finger over his lips.

"Celebrate and be happy this night. Right now, we have a baby. We have good news, raging sex and each other to hold and kiss. That's a blast."

Stroking her breast lightly, he ran his tongue over the curve of her ear and then turned his head to look into her eyes before he kissed her lightly, a sweet kiss. His arm slipped beneath her, drawing her against him and holding her close.

She felt his warm, hard muscles against her, his

arms around her. She was wrapped in his embrace and she kissed his jaw lightly, taking her own advice and not thinking beyond tonight. She reflected on being with his family and how happy they had all looked.

"Ethan must have sensed how happy everyone was with him. He was happy as could be even though I'm the only one there he really knew. I told you—he's a good baby."

"That's because he takes after his dad," Noah said and she laughed.

"That's where he gets his good looks. He gets his good disposition from me."

"I'm still in shock. Maybe this is the best way to find out. No worries and what-ifs about his birth. I love him."

"Noah, I've been thinking since we were with your family. I named Ethan for my uncle Ethan, as you know. My dad was okay with that because he's never liked his name, Mervyn Osbert Warner. He actually asked me not to use his name. I loved Uncle Ethan and spent more time with him and my aunt than I did with my mom and dad. Anyway, I've been thinking. How would you like to change Ethan's middle name to your dad's name? Your dad has a very nice name."

Noah shifted, sitting up slightly to look at her. "You're willing to change?"

"I think I owe you and this is one thing I can do.

Hopefully, it will mean something to your dad. And maybe to you. It would be Ethan Caleb Warner."

Noah slid one arm under her and picked her up to kiss her. After one startled moment, she wrapped her arms around his neck and kissed him in return, and forgot about baby names even when he released her.

Feeling dazed, wanting to pull him back and kiss him again, she looked up at him.

"Thank you, Camilla. I think my dad would feel really great to know he has a little grandson named after him. If you're sure, I can take care of getting it done."

"I'm sure."

He drew her into his arms again, trailing his fingers over her, caressing her with light touches that made her feel cherished and important. She was fascinated by his marvelous body and ran her hands over him, feeling his erection come to life again, which excited her. He shifted, putting his hands on her waist.

"I want to look at you this time," he whispered, pausing to get a condom and put it on. He placed her astride him, entering her, filling her. His hands toyed with her breasts, stroking and caressing her and running his hands over her bottom. She closed her eyes and tossed her head back while he thrust into her and in seconds they pumped wildly together.

"You're beautiful," he said hoarsely, his thrusts making her cry out with pleasure. Caressing him, she rocked with him while tension built. She cried out with need, moving faster, reaching a climax when he did, and together they went over the edge.

When ecstasy enveloped her, she collapsed over him, her hair spreading over his shoulder. He held her tightly with one arm while he slowed and finally was still. His hand stroked her, brushing her long hair from her face, running over her back and down over her bottom.

"You have a fantastic body," he whispered. "Beautiful, so beautiful. So soft. You're a temptation that I dreamed about when I was gone and couldn't be with you." He ran his hands all over her and she clung to him, wishing they could hold the night and everything would be like this with them all the time.

She would do like Noah. Take this moment and not think about tomorrow or what decisions they would have to make. His body was strong, fit, perfect. They had hours for lovemaking and she wanted every minute. She hadn't faced fighting or death or the other things he had overseas, but she'd been alone, and had lost a brother she loved and had a baby without Ethan's father being here or knowing about him.

She wanted a night of passion, hot, thrilling sex and excitement with a man in peak form, muscled, able to love her into oblivion, a man she cared more for than was good for her.

As dawn spilled through the cracks around the closed shutters, Camilla slipped out of bed to open them and then came back to find Noah propped up with his hands behind his head, watching her.

Laughing, she slid beneath the sheet. "I thought you were asleep and wouldn't see me. I'm letting the sunlight in."

"I guarantee you, I'm happy to watch you because you're luscious. See what you do to me with just one glance at you?" he said, taking her hand and placing it on his thick erection.

Her smile vanished as she drew a deep breath and turned to kiss him, and in minutes they made love with her astride him, her eyes closed as she rode him while he pumped hard and fast. When they climaxed at almost the same moment, she cried out with pleasure and fell across him, her long hair spilling over his shoulder. When she slid off to stretch beside him, he pulled her close against him.

"That is the way to wake in the morning," he said.

His voice was a deep rumble. She ran her fingers in the hair on his chest. "I'm going to shower. Ethan will be awake before you know it and he doesn't wait happily for his breakfast. When he wants to eat, he wants to eat."

"Ahh, our adorable son. Thank you again," he said, kissing her lightly.

"You're very welcome," she said, smiling at him.

"I remember you saying you paint early in the morning. Am I ruining your schedule?"

She smiled. "Completely, but there are no complaints. I'm not on a tight deadline here, so it's fine if I miss some mornings."

"That is very good news. I need to get up, too. Although I'd rather spend the day in bed with you, I want to get started on his name change. The sooner the better."

Noah stepped out of bed and her gaze ran over his body that was hard, fit and strong, aroused right now.

"When it comes to sex, you're insatiable," she remarked, looking up to find him watching her.

"That's because you're absolute temptation and keep me constantly aroused. All I have to do is look at you or think about you."

She caught up the sheet and tugged it off the bed to wrap up in it. "Now I'm modestly and properly dressed," she said as she started for the bathroom. "You can shower down the hall. You have your own suite here, remember."

"I remember, but I definitely prefer this one." He blocked her way, smiling at her and wrapping his arms around her. "Want to see how long it takes me to get you immodestly and improperly undressed?"

Laughing, she wriggled, and he let her go. "No way. You go shower—a cold shower to cool you down and I'll see you at breakfast and you can learn how to feed your son. He can do fairly well with parts of breakfast all by himself. It's better to feed him the messy stuff before he puts it in his hair."

"Oh, gross." Noah grimaced. "I'll get dressed in something washable," he said, gathering his clothes.

"This is the part of baby care that mamas do so well and dads need to let them do it."

"Don't you wish. You need this experience. It is definitely part of being a dad."

She hurried past him to head to her bathroom and get ready for the day. Excitement coursed through her and she felt happiness she hadn't known in a long time. Their night of celebration was over and reality would crowd back in and fill their lives, and the sexy, fun relationship they'd had last night would be a memory. All she had to do to keep nights like last night happening was accept Noah the way he was now—a strong alpha male, a rancher, a billionaire who worked at ranching because he loved it. A cowboy country boy through and through, while she was a city girl. If she could accept all that completely, the problems would vanish. She didn't want to live on a ranch, give up her art galleries, opera, stage shows and city life.

As she stepped into the shower, turning on the water, she thought about Noah being such a domineering male. She had grown up promising herself she would never marry an alpha male because of the way her mother had given up a lot of things she wanted to do or did things she didn't want to do because her dad had made all the decisions. She had asked Vivian once how she dealt with being married to the strong-willed man that Thane was. Vivian had her art and she wasn't interested in ranching, yet there she was, living on a ranch because that was what he'd wanted them to do. Vivian had just smiled and said that Thane had made up for doing things his way by doing things for her and she just went ahead and did what she wanted some of the time.

Camilla suspected it was a very small "some of the time." Just the thought of living on a ranch held no appeal. She might try to adjust to that one, but the alpha-male thing—that was his personality. That wasn't going to change one bit.

Camilla showered, washed her hair, dressed in jeans and a short-sleeve blue T-shirt and went to Ethan's bedroom, which adjoined hers. He was standing in his crib and held out his arms when she came inside.

"Mama, up," he said, waving his arms.

"Good morning, my sweet baby," she said, smiling as she lifted him out of the crib. She kissed his rosy cheek. "I love you, Ethan. Today we're going to show your daddy how to feed you breakfast and what you like to eat. You have a smart dad, so he'll get it."

The art showing in Chicago was coming up and it would be wonderful exposure for her art, but it would take her away from Ethan and Noah. She needed to let Noah start taking care of Ethan so he could when she was gone, even though he would have all the help he wanted from her nanny and his family. She knew Stefanie had wanted to get her away from Noah, but that had been before any of them had known about Ethan. Stefanie could not have been nicer last night. Right now, Noah and his family were all enchanted by Ethan. She knew, though, that she and Noah had tough times ahead working out how they would care for Ethan. It scared her to think about it because Noah could be tough and forceful. He wouldn't back down from what he wanted. She couldn't bear to think about sending her little baby off to stay with Noah for any length of time.

Each time Camilla started to rethink her feelings for Noah and his lifestyle, she came right back to the same conclusion. She needed someone in her life who wasn't a rancher, who wasn't such a strong alpha male.

She was going to lose Noah at some point. She was certain he would marry one day. For the next eighteen years at least, they would have to be in touch with each other, sometimes a lot, because of sharing their son. Was she ready for that? Each time she went over that question, the answer was no.

Their problems loomed as big as ever. She hoped that these happy moments they'd spent together would move them toward working out an agreeable arrangement for Ethan. She hoped, but couldn't imagine it happening. The thought of losing her baby half the time tore at her and made her want to lock her door and never see Noah again. Yet when she was with him, they had moments like old times.

Her phone rang and she saw it was the gatekeeper, who said a floral company had a delivery for her.

She told him to send it in. "We're getting pretty flowers that you'd love to eat, but you can't," she cooed at Ethan as she carried him to the front door. "I don't know who is sending them, but we'll know in a minute." She glanced out the sidelight to see a deliveryman taking out a giant bouquet of mixed flowers from his truck. He pulled out another large bouquet of roses. She opened the door and watched as he continued to set gorgeous bouquets out and then he picked up two and carried them to her front door. "Good heavens," she said, glancing at Ethan, who wiggled to get down. "Look, Ethan, we're getting flowers. Lots of flowers."

"Ms. Camilla Warner?" he asked.

"I'm Ms. Warner. You can bring those in here," she said, holding the door open. "Just set them on the table, please."

He went back to get two more vases. She signed that she received them and he left. She walked around looking at roses, lilies, daisies, stalks of blooming ginger, anthurium, gladiolas and tulips. A white teddy bear was in the center of a large blue bow around one vase. She opened the small envelope and removed a card.

You should have had this when Ethan was born. He's wonderful. Noah.

"Look what your nice daddy did. Your very sexy daddy. If it wasn't for you wanting your breakfast, I could go back and thank him for this right now."

Ethan started taking off down the hallway to the kitchen, and she followed.

"Ethan," she said softly, putting him in his high

chair and giving him some little circles of dry cereal to munch while she washed and cut up strawberries for him. She put a little plastic bowl of strawberry slices in front of him. "Now please eat your breakfast so I can go back to bed with your daddy, which is a lot of fun."

"I'll second that suggestion," came a deep voice.

She spun around, feeling her cheeks grow hot as she blushed.

"I should have just wrapped a towel around me and come down and gotten you and Ethan and gone back upstairs. He surely has something that will entertain him," Noah said.

"Unfortunately, he likes people around when he's awake, so no, you can't just send him off to play," she said, feeling tingles as her gaze flicked over him in tight jeans and a fitted black T-shirt that showed his muscles.

She crossed the room to him, put her arms around his neck and looked up at him. "Thank you for the gorgeous flowers. I think they probably had to close the store after filling your order. And I see a teddy bear in it that I assume is for Ethan."

"You assume right. You're welcome."

Noah smiled at her as he put his hands on her waist. "If you can get little one to cooperate and go play with his toys or whatever he does, then we can go back to bed."

"You weren't listening a minute ago. He has no intention of entertaining himself. Quite often, he gets his way."

"That's not fair because I damn sure don't."

"Are we going to start the day with a fight?" she asked sweetly.

"No, we're not. We'll start with me getting to feel how soft you are, check how great you smell," he said, inhaling, "and see if you can still be as sexy to kiss in the early morning as you were in the night." He kissed away any answer she may have had.

He held her close against him as he kissed her passionately, leaning over her until she clung to him and kissed him in return. By the time he released her, she gulped for air.

"It can be so damn good between us," Noah said.

"Yes, it can," she agreed. "But we have some big decisions to make and some big problems to work around," she said, studying him intently. What they'd shared last night and just now hadn't solved anything, and had pulled them a little closer together— and would make it hurt more if they couldn't work things out.

"I have to get his breakfast," Camilla said, passing Noah. "You can watch and learn," she added.

"After that kiss, right now, there's only one person I can watch. You watch him and I'll focus on your gorgeous body and think about how it felt against mine."

She pulled out a container of rolled oats and poured some into a bowl with water. "He's messy with oatmeal, and when he's not hungry, he uses the spoon to throw food around. I try to anticipate that and take his spoon away from him."

"I don't suppose telling him no does any good."

"It makes him laugh."

"I don't think you know how to be forceful."

She turned to look at Noah. "Uh-huh. I want to see this. You'll melt like hot butter when he starts smiling at you."

"He learned that from you."

"I don't believe I see you giving in to me on a regular basis."

"Maybe you're not using the right enticement. Now, last night, you could have gotten anything you wanted."

"We weren't going to do this," she said, and his smile was gone.

"I had high hopes for this celebration lasting a while."

"Noah, you know we're just setting ourselves up for a bigger hurt."

"We've already hurt each other, so that would be nothing new. In the meantime, relax. Celebrate with me for a few days. We might work better together later." He grinned again and she could feel herself weakening.

"You owe me this, Camilla. I didn't get to celebrate when he was born and you did."

She shook her head as she smiled. "Noah, you're

manipulating me, but you know I can't say no to that one."

"Good." He leaned closer and slipped his hand to her nape, caressing her lightly and stirring desire. "I think you like celebrating with me."

"You know I do," she whispered, looking at his mouth, and then he kissed her. His arms wrapped around her and her heart pounded as he kissed her possessively.

"In some ways it's very good between us. We're good together."

Her heart missed a beat as she gazed into his blue eyes. "Yes, we are."

"Look, just come look at my ranch. Let me take Ethan and you and come see the place. It's not going to be one bit like your grandfather's."

She drew a deep breath. "Noah, there's just no point in it."

He frowned slightly. "Camilla, we have moments that are good. We have moments that are fun. The sex couldn't be better. We could be a family now."

"Yes, we can if I would compromise and do everything the way you want. I don't hear you offering to live in Dallas."

"I am what I am, Camilla. I'd be lying if I said I'd change. I don't consciously think 'I'm an alpha male, so I'll take charge.' There are just a lot of times someone needs to take charge and so I do. We're both strong-willed. You can't tell me you're not."

"I know," she said. "I am who I am. I can't change and neither can you."

He placed his hands on her shoulders. "We have a big reason to try to stay together. Come for just a couple of days and see my ranch."

She took a deep breath and thought about last night in his arms.

She looked at Ethan and knew she had to do what she could to work with Noah. "Let me think about it."

Noah smiled. "Thank you. Look at your calendar. You know I'm free. Right now, I'm going to call my attorney and get his middle name change started. We'll have to go to court, I'm sure. Later today I'll get some of my things moved over here." He left the room and she shook her head as she turned to give Ethan more of the slices of strawberries.

"I think your daddy just wiggled out of feeding you breakfast today. I think he's going to change your life and mine a lot. I know you'll be happy with what he does. I can just hope for the best for all of us." As she heated up his oatmeal, she told him, "It looks like we're going to a ranch. You'll probably like it."

But would she?

Honestly, she felt she owed Noah some favors for not telling him about Ethan sooner, but extending this celebration would just make it hurt more than ever when they parted, and they definitely would part. He hadn't declared he was in love or even suggested marriage. She hadn't changed her feelings, either. She didn't want a ranch life and she definitely didn't want a lifetime of dealing with another strong-willed male. Yet this time with Noah made her realize one more thing. One thing that presented an insurmountable problem.

She hadn't gotten over him at all.

Eight

Camilla

During the morning Camilla received another call from the art gallery in Chicago, and when she finished, she booked a flight to Chicago.

She had left Noah in the nursery with Ethan and she wondered how things were going. She went to find them.

Surprisingly he was in the backyard, standing beneath a big oak while Ethan sat in the grass. "What are you doing?"

"I thought he needed to be outside. Does he have a swing?"

"No, he doesn't. I never thought about a swing."

"They have baby swings and we can fasten him

in and he'll love it. This tree is perfect. I'll get one today and put it up. You'll see. He'll like to swing and you'll like having a swing for him."

"Okay." She leaned down and handed Ethan the ball that had gotten away from him. Then she looked back at Noah. "I made my flight arrangements for Chicago to see the art-gallery people. They're really eager to show my paintings and I need to go talk to them. I owe your sister thanks, even though I know she did it to get me away from you."

He shook his head. "I think she'll stop. Frankly, I think she wants us together now because of Ethan," he said and gave Camilla a big smile.

"I know she loves you and she seemed truly thrilled over Ethan."

"She is," Noah said, glancing at Ethan, who was now happily pulling out grass. "She wants to keep him sometime and I told her she could."

"That's nice, Noah. He has a wonderful family with your family."

"Good."

"Now, while I'm shopping for baby furniture, do you want me to get my nanny to take care of Ethan, or would you like to take care of him?" They'd already agreed that Camilla would outfit a nursery for his Dallas condo.

"Let me," Noah replied. "I'll get my folks if I have difficulty. I may just stay right here because you're set up for a baby. I'm glad I'm going to start getting my condo that way." He pulled out his wallet. "Here's my credit card."

She took it and slipped it into her pocket.

"I've been thinking," he said. "Whatever you buy, get two, and we'll have the second one shipped to the ranch and set up there."

"You want it all alike?"

"Yes, because Ethan won't care and I don't. And it'll be easier for you. Later when he outgrows the baby stuff, we can do something more original."

She shook her head. When Ethan outgrew the baby furniture, she would probably not be the one buying furniture on Noah's behalf. It might be his wife—a thought that she didn't like to consider.

She looked at Noah standing in the shade, looking up at the tree, his thick black curls in their usual appealing tangle. He was all hard muscles from his head to his feet, handsome, sexy and exciting. She wanted to be in his arms, but that was putting off reality and the problems they needed to solve. Right now those problems seemed monumental and without a happy solution. When they parted this time, after being together with Ethan, she suspected it would hurt more than it had the first time when he left for the Army.

She forced herself to abandon that line of thinking and focus on the task at hand. "Okay. Two sets of furniture it is. Just one question—can you clear enough space for a suite for him in your condo now?"

"I've been thinking about that. Go ahead and buy it, so it's all selected, and tell them I'll call and give them an address to deliver it to. I may get them to hold part of the order and just buy a house here so we'll have a yard. I can get my brothers and Stefanie to find some likely houses for me fast."

"There's one for sale a block south of here. Then we'd be in the same neighborhood and it would make sharing Ethan easier."

"Give me the address and I'll ask about it and look at it. It won't take long for me to make a decision."

"They have a sign in the front yard. I have a listing for this area. I'll leave the name of the current owners, the address and their phone number on the kitchen table for you."

"Good."

"I'm leaving now. You're sure you'll be okay with him?"

Noah nodded. "We'll be fine."

She left him with Ethan and spent the next hours selecting baby furniture for the ranch and for Noah to have in Dallas.

All the time she did, she was aware she was setting up a nursery and a playroom for Ethan, but she wouldn't be with him when he was with his dad.

It was almost five when she returned that afternoon. While she had been shopping, she had been in touch with Noah by phone and text, and he'd assured her they were doing fine. When she got back to her house, she found him putting together a baby swing. But no sign of their son.

"Ethan is at my folks'," he explained. "I'll go get

him whenever you want or we have a dinner invitation, thanks to Ethan."

"Whatever you want to do. I'll be happy to see your family again."

He picked up the baby swing he'd finished. "Now I'll put this in the tree. C'mon. You can hand me stuff. Did you get the furniture?"

"I think I did—two of everything and the furniture will be delivered this Thursday to the ranch. They will hold the rest here until we give them an address and instructions where to deliver it."

"Thank you. C'mon," he said, carrying the baby swing and rope outside to the tree.

"You need a ladder."

"No, I don't," he said, jumping up and grabbing a limb. He caught it easily. She watched him swing himself up and climb to the next limb, muscles flexing as he moved with ease, proving how fit he was. He had two lengths of rope looped around his shoulder and in minutes he had one end of each length around a branch with a length of rubber from an old garden hose to protect the tree. He knotted each length and dropped to the ground, landing on his feet. He inserted the ends of each length of rope in the back of the swing and secured them with knots. "Now he has a swing."

Noah turned to look at her and then arched an eyebrow as her gaze ran over his chest and she drew a deep breath. His hand closed on her arm and he stepped close to put his arm around her.

"Noah, we're outside."

"There's no one here except us and this is your house with a high fence, bushes and trees and all the privacy in the world. When you look at me the way you just did, there's no way I can resist kissing you," he said. He kissed away an answer, picking her up while he kissed her.

She wound her arms around his neck, holding him and kissing him in return. She tingled from head to toe. Noah was sexy, incredibly appealing with solid muscles, fit and agile. In spite of all the differences and problems between them, she wanted to be in bed with him, all that strength and energy turned to blazing sex. She moaned softly, her breasts tingling, wanting his hands and mouth on her and his body against hers.

She wasn't aware of her surroundings until he let her stand in his bedroom as he peeled away her clothes and she removed his.

"You have an incredible body," she whispered, running her fingers over him, feeling his rock-hard chest.

"Baby," he whispered, "that's my line. You definitely have the incredible body and I can't ever get enough. In bed is where we're in total and absolute agreement."

He showered kisses across her belly, his one hand caressing her breast as his other hand made feather strokes along the inside of first one thigh and then the other. The light, slow brushes of his warm fingers moved up slowly until they touched her intimately, and she gasped.

He covered her mouth, kissing her deeply, sensations bombarding her, sizzling torment making her want all of him. His hand continued to tease her nipple and stroke between her legs, making her want more.

In minutes, he laid her on the bed and got a condom. As soon as he had it on, he moved over her to enter her. She clung to him, lost to sensation, and nearly immediately reached a climax. She held him tightly, knowing soon he would leave her arms, leave her bed and, all too soon, leave an emptiness in her heart.

The first of the week Noah went with his dad to meet his doctor and Noah sat through the exam. To his relief, the report had been positive. His father wasn't going to get over the heart trouble, but they could keep it stable and his dad comfortable. Noah felt free to ask questions, and then when they left, Noah stepped back briefly to ask some direct questions about his dad's outlook. He joined his dad in the waiting room and relayed what he had learned that was positive. He felt better about his dad. He would be less worried going to the ranch when he finally decided to do so. Now, with Ethan in his life and his family so delighted to have him around, Noah felt he needed to stay in Dallas for a while longer. He had to admit, Camilla held him in Dallas and he didn't want to question too closely how important she was becoming to him because they had such huge differences that had not only never changed, but now became even more important with Ethan in their lives. They had a baby now and the nights with her were magic. Could they ever reconcile their differences?

A few days later Noah and Camilla stood in the empty courtroom and had Ethan's name officially changed to Ethan Caleb Warner.

When they left the courtroom with the offical papers in Noah's hand, he glanced down the empty hall and drew her to him.

Startled, she looked up at him.

"Thank you for doing that. It will mean so much to my dad and my family and it does to me." He kissed her briefly and Camilla smiled at him.

"Wait until we're home and I'll really thank you," he said, slipping his arm across her shoulders as they turned to leave.

That evening they were invited to Noah's parents' house for dinner for a celebration of the name change. It was a warm night and they'd planned a cookout.

They went to their suite to change, and a half hour later Camilla heard him knock on her closed door. She was in the en suite putting her hair in a ponytail while Ethan was sitting on the floor in her bedroom playing with his toys. She called out for Noah to enter.

"Hey, little buddy, come here," she heard him say as he came in. "You look very spiffy in your light blue jumper. I hope you can stay that way for an hour so all the folks will be impressed by how cute you are."

"Dada," she heard Ethan say, followed by Noah calling out, "Hey, Camilla, he called me daddy."

She came out of the en suite laughing and shaking her head as she saw Ethan in his arms. "I heard. I've been trying to teach him to say 'Daddy.'"

"'Dada' is close enough," Noah said. When he looked at her she suddenly wanted the evening to be over and to be back home with him. He looked so handsome in navy slacks and a pale blue shirt open at the throat.

She felt him rake his gaze over her red cotton summer dress. "I have my hands filled with baby or I'd come kiss you. You look fantastic," he said.

She smiled at him. "I was about to say the same. My goodness, you are a handsome man."

"Let's go get this evening over with so I can carry you off to bed," he said, sounding as if he was barely able to get his breath.

Her smile vanished. "Noah, what are we going to do? We've got this intense attraction that neither of us can resist. We have a precious baby between us. At the same time, we're polar opposites in lifestyles and temperament."

His smile disappeared and she regretted putting a damper on the moment. But it was the truth. And it hurt. She knew what she was losing when they really split apart. This was just a brief, temporary truce because of Ethan. None of her basic feelings had changed, but Noah's appeal was intensifying. She was headed for a huge heartbreak.

"I can't give you an answer, Camilla. I am what I am. I know we have a physical relationship that's fantastic. I think about you constantly and I'm instantly filled with desire when I see you. I don't have an answer for how we can work out a relationship where we're both happy. It's that simple. At the same time, the attraction continues to grow. At least for me. I've told you that family is everything and I want one. We're halfway there."

"Noah, other than the fact we have a baby, we're not even close to halfway there."

He frowned. "Family is important to me. It's a high priority. And it involves commitment, deep love, sharing, making adjustments, and right now, we don't have that. Being together, some of that might come. It sure as hell won't come if we're totally separated. And you were right about me moving in with you being the best way to learn how to take care of Ethan. I want us to be his mom and dad and be together, but that won't work unless we have those things I just mentioned— love, commitment, adjustments. There's no point in getting into a relationship that isn't going to work and you know it."

"Yes, I do," she replied, hurting, feeling as if the gulf between them just widened when he stated all those qualities of a strong relationship and announced they didn't have any of them. "You're right. Without love, marriage isn't going to work."

She hurt badly and just wanted to walk into his arms and hold him tightly and have him offer some small changes, but she knew that was a dream. Maybe she should think about what she could change. The minute that thought came, she thought how her mother had spent a lifetime changing what she wanted in order to shift her life to what Camilla's dad wanted.

She slipped on the gold bracelet Thane had sent home to her and held out her arm. "Look, here's what my brother asked you to bring to me."

Noah took her wrist in his warm grasp. "That's beautiful." He looked up at her and slipped his hand lightly on her nape. "And so are you," he said, his voice getting a rasp. "And this is a good moment—here's a gift from me this time," he said, reaching into his pocket and withdrawing a small box.

Surprised, she took the box and looked at him.

"Go ahead—open it. That's for Ethan, for the name change."

She opened the box and removed a small jewelry box and snapped it open. "Noah," she said, picking up a gold chain with a sparkling diamond pendant. "It's beautiful. Thank you," she said, knowing she would treasure his gift just as she did her brother's, but with Noah, she couldn't fathom his true feelings. Was the gift purely gratitude for Ethan—or did Noah feel anything deeper?

"Put it on me. I'm wearing it tonight," she said, putting the necklace in his hand, turning and lifting her hair. She felt his warm fingers brush her nape.

"There," he said.

She turned to look into his blue eyes that were filled with desire. She stood on tiptoe, slipped her arm around his neck and kissed him.

Instantly, his arm circled her waist as they kissed.

She wiggled away. "Thank you. I'll thank you more later. Right now we better go." She started packing all the things she would take for Ethan, although she suspected someone would play with him every second of the evening. Noah's family had seemed enchanted by him the last time they were with them.

Her guess proved correct as every member of Noah's family had to hold him when they arrived.

She had to show everyone her necklace from Noah because of Ethan and her bracelet that Thane sent home to her.

Before dinner she stood on the veranda close to Betsy and Cal, who were seated. Cal held Ethan and they both played with him and talked to him. Camilla was talking with Stefanie and Hallie while Noah and his brothers hung out across the veranda.

Camilla thought about what a wonderful family the Grants had, and now Ethan would be one of them. She felt another pang of longing to be with Noah, to be part of this family and to have that for Ethan. It hurt more today to hear Noah talk about love and commitment when he had never come close to indicating he loved her or that he wanted to make a commitment. She hadn't either, but it was because he hadn't.

She had to admit, she was probably as determined

and strong-willed as Noah, and that wasn't a good combination. Neither one could change a basic personality. She looked at Noah, who was laughing at something Ben said. Noah's gaze shifted and met hers and she felt as if he'd touched her.

Looking into his blue eyes always made her pulse beat faster at first glance. Noah was a force to be reckoned with—absolutely the most desirable man she had ever known. Her insides knotted because she was pained with wanting him. Too much of the day she hurt over the thought of Noah leaving her life. She had made one mistake in a relationship—marrying a man to try to get over Noah. She didn't want to make another big mistake here and lose the love of her life. And she did love him. Years ago she had never told him because she didn't think he loved her. They hadn't talked about marriage and now she didn't think he ever would. Had she made a big mistake then by not visiting his ranch and at least trying to see if they could work things out?

His gaze still held hers, which surprised her. What was going through his thoughts? Did he hurt the way she did?

Then Ben must have said something directly to him and he turned back to his brother.

They had dinner and she sat between Stefanie and Hallie, across from Noah's parents, who flanked Ethan's high chair. They obviously relished every moment they spent with the baby. Noah sat at the other end of the table, with his brothers.

She hadn't spoken a word to him all evening and she couldn't help but feel as if a wall had come back between them. But why?

After dinner, she found him in the den, deep in conversation with Ben. He looked up and walked over to her in the doorway. "Camilla, we need to talk," he said, leading her into an empty adjacent room.

"Is everything okay?" she asked him.

He nodded, but his eyes didn't meet hers when he spoke. "I've been thinking about us. I can think more clearly when we're not just the two of us—then I get sidetracked and want to kiss you." He took a deep breath… "Sooner or later, we're going to have to come to grips with how we'll share Ethan. And it will have to be official. I don't want a handshake deal. I want an agreement in court that is legal and binding. I want joint custody and I want him half the time."

Half the time? Joint custody with Noah? He had told her that before, but he was emphatic about it now. Pain gripped her heart like a vise and she had to fight back tears because they had to face all his family as soon as they walked out of this room.

"I understand," she said, certain that Noah wasn't going to be easy to deal with. She had known this was coming, but it still hurt to hear him state his demands. She knew for certain Noah would fight for what he wanted.

Right now she couldn't face this. She couldn't even look at him.

"I'll join you in a few minutes, Noah," she said,

turning to go to a bathroom where she could close the door and have privacy.

She leaned against the door and wiped at the tears that spilled out. They had been getting along and she didn't know what made him think about the future, but the time would come soon when they would go their separate ways, and when it did, they had to make arrangements to share Ethan and she was going to hurt more than she ever had in her life. She loved her son and she loved Noah. She would lose Noah and she wouldn't have Ethan half the time. Half of all the time he was growing up. That sounded unbearable.

Because of his dad's health, she knew she wouldn't have to deal with Noah leaving Dallas for a while, and she tried to focus on that and push worries out of her mind, at least until she was home and away from his family. Taking a deep breath, she left the bathroom and went back to join them in the great room. When Stefanie saw her from across the room she shot Camilla a long look. She wondered if Noah had told his sister he was unhappy. Camilla knew little sister Stefanie was protective of her older brother; it was written all over her face.

Before she could go speak to Stefanie, Noah came over. "I think Ethan will crash soon. Are you ready to leave?"

"Sure," she said, gathering their things.

It was another half hour before they had said their goodbyes and were in the car. The minute Noah started driving down the long circle drive, Ethan was asleep in his car seat.

"My dad is so happy with Ethan and he's over the moon with having him named Ethan Caleb Warner. That was a wonderful gesture," Noah said.

"You have a wonderful family and that makes me happy for Ethan."

"They all love him, that's for sure," Noah said. She watched him drive, looking at his handsome profile, the dark curls falling on his forehead. In spite of the differences between them, in spite of their eventual joint custody of their son, she couldn't deny her attraction to him. Neither could she deny that she wanted to be in his arms.

He was incredibly handsome, more so than he had been before he had gone into the Army. She had already faced the fact that she was in love with him and headed straight for disaster, but tonight, if he wanted to make love, she'd step right into his arms.

Later, when she was in bed in his arms, she shifted so she could look at him. "Noah, I thought of something else. I'd like to have Ethan christened while your dad is able to attend and enjoy the event."

Noah rolled on his side and propped his head on his hand. "That would be great. I hadn't given that a thought, and guessed you had already had him christened."

"No. By the time Ethan was born, I missed you being here—I just put it off. Once I started putting it off, it was easy to continue to do so. Now would be a good time."

"My folks would really like it." Noah placed his palm gently on her cheek. "Naming him after Dad, christening him so Dad can attend—you are doing a lot for me and for my family."

"I think I owe you," she said quietly, her heart beating harder because she wanted everything to work out between them and it never could. "Noah, I'm trying. I want to work things out between us for Ethan's sake," she admitted. She couldn't change the basic issues she had about Noah being such an alpha male and being a cowboy. It didn't matter about the money—rich or poor or anywhere in between, a cowboy at heart was a cowboy and wealth or lack of it didn't matter. In spite of his fortune Noah was a rancher and a cowboy. The more they were together like tonight, the more she was going to be hurt in the future. When he walked out of her life, would she ever stop missing him?

He pulled her close to kiss her tenderly and she wrapped her arms around him, holding him tightly, knowing she would lose him and wondering if she would love him all her life.

"I don't suppose you've thought about working in Dallas and giving up the ranch?" she asked him. "You're living here anyway."

He rolled back to look at her again. "No. I'm a rancher and my dad is doing okay. I've talked to his doctors. I've been gone so much the last three years I needed to see the folks, and now with Ethan, that's all the more reason to extend my stay in Dallas, but eventually, I'm going to my ranch. I want you to come see it, Camilla. If you will, that would be good news."

She gazed into his unfathomable blue eyes. Why was he pushing her to visit his ranch? Hope blossomed in her heart. Did that mean his feelings toward her were changing, becoming more serious?

Noah had never declared love and neither had she. She'd felt she loved him before he joined the military, but it was not enough to overlook what she didn't like. What she felt for him had grown stronger since he had learned about Ethan. Now that Noah had learned he was the father of her baby, he had done all the right things. He had been filled with joy over the news, sorry he hadn't been with her, instantly joyous and loving his baby, taking Ethan and her to introduce their son to his family, and later celebrating just the two of them, a smoking-hot, passionate celebration of the birth of his son. He was irresistible in so many ways, but then there was the other side—the alpha male. She would not follow in her mother's footsteps and fall in love with one then spend a lifetime with a man who made all her decisions for her.

Especially since she was not like her mother. She could be as stubborn as Noah, which meant they'd probably butt heads every step of the way. She would know more about how they could work together when they started working out custody of Ethan. Just the thought of that gave her a chill. She was going to lose her baby part of the time.

And she had no idea about the depth of Noah's

feelings for her. He had never given any indication of being in love, much less that he wanted anything permanent. And she still didn't think they could ever work past the problems.

Yet if she was falling more deeply in love with him and if there was a shred of hope to work out custody of Ethan without a battle and heartbreak, she should go see his ranch. A few days in the country wasn't much. She could do that, just visit. After all, she wanted Noah in her life—but on her terms. The realization shocked her. She turned to look at him as he lay beside her on the bed, running her finger along his jawline, feeling tickles from the black stubble on his jaw.

"Noah, I'll visit your ranch," she said, and he shifted, propping his head on his hand to look at her.

"You and Ethan will go home with me?" She heard the surprise in his voice and he was staring intently at her.

"You've asked me several times. You and I are sharing Ethan now and that means we will be in each other's lives to some extent for at least the next sixteen or so years. I should at least have enough of an open mind to accept your invitation to visit."

He gazed solemnly at her and she wondered what he was thinking. He leaned over and wrapped his arms around her, sat up and lifted her to his lap.

"You always surprise me," he said. "There will never be another surprise as big as Ethan, but this is a surprise and I'm glad. Even if you hate the place, at least you'll have been there. That's good, Camilla. That's called an open mind."

"Don't be a smart aleck and don't push your luck."

He studied her and she had no idea what ran through his thoughts until he pulled her to him to kiss her. In minutes they rolled down on the bed and he caressed her, running his hand lightly over her, and she forgot everything. Everything except desire.

Sunday, they stood at the front of the church while the minister and assistant pastor went through the christening ceremony of Ethan Caleb Warner while Noah's family and Camilla's family stood with them. Afterward, they all went to the country club where Noah had a private room reserved and dinner catered.

It was three in the afternoon before Noah, Camilla and Ethan went back to Camilla's house. Ethan was asleep and Noah carried him to his crib, standing and looking down at his son.

Camilla came in and stood in the doorway watching Noah. When she finally joined him, he put his arm around her.

"He's still a marvel to me. I just can't believe I'm a dad. He's a super son. He was so happy and good today and everyone loved playing with him."

"Were you half that good?" she asked. "And don't say, 'Of course.'"

He smiled. "Let's get out of here before we push our luck too far and wake him." He ushered her out of the nursery. "To answer your question, no, I can't recall great praise about what a happy, good baby I was. Don't ask me questions like that. Ask Mom."

"I'll bet you were born giving orders."

"I'm not that bossy."

She shot him a look that told him she didn't believe that for a second. They started walking down the hall. "You remember that I leave tomorrow for Chicago, right? I'll be back Tuesday. Are you going to stay here or at your mom's?"

"I plan to stay here. I can take care of a little baby until your return."

She smiled. "Well, you know where to get help if you need it. We still have the nanny on call, even if we've never had her out here since you moved in."

He took her hand in his. "Come with me," he said and walked her into his bedroom. "The monitor is on, Ethan is sound asleep and all's quiet on the home front. I've waited way too long and you'll be gone tomorrow night," he said as he wrapped his arms around her and leaned down to kiss her.

She slipped her arms around his neck, kissing him in return, reveling in the moment, knowing that all too soon now, Noah would move on and her life would change again—a forever change—without Ethan half the time. The thought suddenly struck her. Was she cheating their son out of a family because she disliked the country? She might be getting ahead of herself because Noah had never told her he loved her, much less talked about commitment. He loved his ranch so much, he might not want commitment from someone who didn't love it the way he did.

He raised his head to look at her. "Something wrong?"

She looked into curious blue eyes. "You're too perceptive sometimes. I was thinking about us."

"I'll try to keep your mind more on us," he said, leaning forward to kiss her again.

As desire swamped her, she forgot their problems. She wrapped her arms tightly around his waist and kissed him back. Then she stepped back to unbutton her blouse as he watched her.

She unbuttoned it and then reached out to unfasten his belt. He shed his shirt and jeans quickly, and then she walked into his arms and stopped worrying about their future.

Nine

Noah

Noah turned into Camilla's drive and parked, smiling when he saw her car. She was home from Chicago and he was glad. He'd missed her. He was happier when they were together, which made him examine his feelings for her. He had never gotten over her, not even after their big blowup before he went into the Army and not after three years when he'd seen her only once.

The first time he had seen her when he returned, his heart had felt as if it would pound out of his chest and desire had been a flash fire sweeping over him. That reaction hadn't changed.

But he didn't want to lock himself into a marriage

that wouldn't work. That would be worse for his son than no marriage between his parents. Noah knew they could be compatible, but they also were two strong-willed people who could dig their heels in and refuse to cooperate with each other.

Family had always been all-important to him. He loved his family and wanted his own to be as harmonious. That took some work and giving. His mother gave big-time, to his way of thinking, but she made that marriage work. And she was happy. He felt certain about that. He didn't know if he could have that with Camilla. He didn't want to live in Dallas and work in the family business and be a suit. He loved the ranch and ranching. That was a divide between them that he couldn't overlook or bridge.

She couldn't accept his being an alpha male and he didn't know any possible way he could change that one if he wanted to in the worst way.

He didn't know the sum of his feelings for Camilla because he always came up against these two problems in their relationship and it stopped him cold. She would never marry him as long as these two things were part of her life or his. They had to be worked out before he could ever truly love her enough for a big commitment. Which might keep them from ever being a family. That hurt, but it would hurt more if they married and then were unhappy and divorced. He didn't want to make a mistake that would hurt his future and his baby's future.

He walked in the door. "Honey, I'm home," he called.

Smiling, she came out of the library and his heart-beat quickened again. She wore a short, straight navy business skirt that made her legs look great, and a matching blouse. Gold bangles were on her wrist and she had her hair looped and fastened on the back of her head.

"You're gorgeous, and did I ever miss you."

She walked into his embrace and put her arms around his neck. "I'm glad, because I missed you," she said without smiling at him.

"Something wrong?"

She shook her head. "No. Just that we're not always going to be together."

"Pretend for tonight. Mom and Dad wanted to keep Ethan again tonight and I told them yes, because I want to be alone with you," he admitted, nuzzling her neck, inhaling her perfume, glad she was in his arms.

"I'd think your mom might be getting a little tired of him."

"Are you kidding? Hallie has been there the whole time and she and Ben slept over there last night to be with him, and they might again tonight. Stefanie loves to play with him and rock him. It's a wonder Eli didn't come over, too, but...well, he thinks he's a cute little kid, but Eli likes his peace and quiet at night, or his girlfriends."

"I'm glad Hallie and Stefanie are there because they have more energy and they can help your mom."

"How was your trip? Is the art show on?"

"Actually, it is. It will be in October, a while away, but they book ahead. Once I show there, they will keep my art on display for six months."

"I'm glad it went well."

"It did except I missed you and Ethan."

He leaned down to kiss her, but she pulled back. "Noah, let's talk about our situation," she said, stepping out of his arms. "Sit, and let's talk."

He wanted to carry her to his bed, but realizing she looked concerned, he nodded.

She sat in a straight-back Queen Anne chair and he sat facing her, aware she wasn't sitting on the sofa where he could touch and hold her. Even her voice sounded tight when she spoke.

"We were going to celebrate the night you learned about Ethan. One night. We're still together—which I'm happy about, but I feel sort of in limbo. We're not really off and we're not really on. You're here under the same roof to learn how to deal with Ethan, but that didn't include sleeping together, which we're doing."

He leaned toward her and took her hand. "Have you ever heard that old expression 'Go with the flow'? For right now that's what we're doing. I'm learning to be a dad and getting to know my baby."

"Before I drop the matter, I don't think you've disliked being here in Dallas with Ethan and me," she said, and immediately he knew she was going to talk to him about living and working in Dallas, which he did not want to do. And right now, she was inches away, and she had been away since the night before last. They could come back to the problems, but he wanted her now.

"Let it go for tonight, Camilla. I missed you too much to get into a discussion about our future." He kissed away her answer, pulling her up against him. His hand went to the hem of her skirt and slipped her skirt up, sliding up and caressing her legs.

"Damn, I missed you," he whispered. His fingers now worked the buttons of her blouse and soon he pushed it off her shoulders and leaned back slightly to unfasten her lacy bra and toss it away. He cupped her breasts and rubbed her nipples lightly.

She gasped and cried out. "Noah, I want you," she whispered.

She tugged free his belt buckle and unfastened his jeans, freeing him in minutes, her fingers moving frantically.

She stroked his manhood, caressing him, kneeling to run her tongue over him, almost sending him over the edge. He wanted to take time, to pleasure her until she was as desperate to make love as he was. But he couldn't wait. He needed her now. He yanked away her panties and then lifted her high to stroke her nipple with his tongue, and then he lowered her onto his erection. She locked her legs around him and they moved together. She clung to him with her eyes closed and her head thrown back, her long hair swinging while he pumped fast. Her hands on him tightened and she cried out as she climaxed, but instead of slowing, she kept thrusting her hips, shifting wildly until she reached another climax.

In minutes she clung to his shoulders, lowered her legs and stood. "Hold me," she whispered. "I feel as if I'm going to melt."

"You're fantastic," he whispered, caressing her, showering light kisses on her forehead.

He picked her up to carry her to the shower, where he peeled away his socks and boots and her shoes. He stood her on her feet and turned on the warm water. His hands were all over her, caressing her, sliding over her curves. And in seconds, he was hard.

"Noah, you're insatiable and you're strong enough to do this all night long."

"Let's see if you're right."

At dawn she fell asleep again in his arms and later woke to roll over and run her hand lightly over him.

He was aroused and she kissed his shoulder. "You never stop."

"It's because I'm with you." He turned to look at her, smiling, slipping his arm around her.

"This isn't the real world."

"Shh. Enjoy today. I promise, the real world will come in time. I keep hoping for a miracle. I want you in my bed."

She started to answer and he kissed her, ending their conversation because this situation wouldn't last and they hadn't solved anything between them.

When he awakened, an hour had passed. He held Camilla close against his side. She was warm, soft, her skin smooth and silky. He wondered how deep her feelings for him ran. Neither of them had ever declared love, and love was the game-changer. Love made all the difference.

They needed to talk and get out of this limbo that couldn't last. When he got a chance, when Ethan was asleep so they wouldn't be interrupted, he wanted to talk to her about the future. It was time for him to move on. He dreaded it, but it might as well happen. He didn't want to hurt her, nor did he want to be hurt, but they needed to get on with their lives.

Camilla

It was morning when she stirred and looked around the empty bed and could smell something enticing emanating from the kitchen.

She rolled out of bed, grabbed a robe and went to her bath to shower. Twenty minutes later she walked into the kitchen.

In a T-shirt and tight jeans, Noah stood there stirring something in a skillet. There were two glasses of orange juice on the table.

She crossed the room and slid her arms around his waist to hug him. "Good morning, very sexy man," she said, unable to resist him even when she knew every caress, each kiss would just make saying goodbye worse when the time came.

"Hey," he said, turning and putting down a spatula. "You look and smell good." He wrapped his arms around her and kissed her.

When he released her, she felt dazed.

"I just need to eat to maintain my strength to keep up with you."

"Breakfast and maybe then bed. Want an omelet? I make the best one ever."

"You're so modest. We need to work on your lack of confidence," she teased. "Of course I want one of your delicious omelets." She poured two cups of coffee and carried them to the table and in minutes he came with a platter that held the golden omelets. Bowls of blueberries and sliced strawberries and kiwi were on the table, as well as toasted wheat bread.

He sat facing her. "I could get very used to this, Camilla." He looked serious and sounded sincere. She couldn't stop the words that hurtled from her mouth.

"Settle in the city, Noah."

She felt as if a barrier appeared between them the moment he turned away. "This might please you," he said. "Eli has found three houses in this neighborhood that I have appointments to look at today. You're welcome to look with me if you want."

Her heart missed a beat. Would he possibly get a house in town and give up the ranch or would it simply be a replacement for his condo? "I'd love to look with you. Whatever happens, I'm thrilled you're looking for a house in this neighborhood."

"Don't get too excited. I'll always have a place to live in Dallas and I'll always spend some time here.

Just not most of the time. I'll pick Ethan up this morning and bring him home. I imagine he's worn my folks down by now. Let's talk about going to the ranch. Neither of us has anything in particular scheduled right away, right?"

"Yes, I'm free."

"Good. I'll call to get the house ready. How about going the day after tomorrow? We can spend the weekend there. Better yet, stay a few days into the week so you can see what it's like."

"That's fine with me, Noah."

He leaned closer and placed his hand on her waist. "I'm glad you'll visit the ranch."

"You expect me to love it, don't you?"

"I hope you do. It's my way of life. That isn't going to change, Camilla."

"Noah, we've never talked about a future together."

His blue eyes darkened and his hand tightened slightly on her waist. "No, we haven't, but we're sharing a child now and we've shared a bed plenty of times and it's been damn fabulous. If we could work out the problems, then we might have a future to talk about. We don't now," he said bluntly, and a pain enveloped her.

"I've told you, family is all-important to me, and there has to be certain things for a family to function well. It won't work for us to marry and you live in Dallas while I live at the ranch. That wouldn't do a bit of good for Ethan. Or for us. There has to be real love, deep and strong. We have a lot of strong feelings for each other, but with the problems, we're not there yet on unconditional love. If we marry for the wrong reasons, it won't last, and I don't want that hurt. We just need to keep trying to work things out until we do or until we know for certain that we never will. Then we say goodbye and figure out how to share Ethan."

His blue eyes were icy. Noah had his moments when he was unyielding. This was one of them.

"I'm willing to try, Noah. That's why I agreed to visit your ranch."

"I'm glad. That's a first step. We'll just see how that goes."

Camilla reached across the table and put her hand over his. "If only it could stay this way, Noah. We can do so well together and Ethan would have a mama and a daddy."

When his surprise changed to a shuttered look, she withdrew her hand.

"Right now I'm in the city 24/7 but I won't be much longer. This is to get to know Ethan, to learn how to care for him, to let him become accustomed to me and being around my family. Staying year-round—that's not going to happen," he said, and she heard that unyielding tone that she had heard before.

"I'll go pick Ethan up and leave him with you if that's convenient."

"Yes, it is."

"Before I go to my folks' house, I have an appointment this morning with my attorney, Camilla."

She gazed into his unyielding blue eyes and a cold chill gripped her because she was afraid they were headed for a court custody fight. "You don't think we can work this out between us?"

"You tell me. You don't like ranch life and I'm too much the alpha male for you."

All their closeness from the past days diminished.

"Noah, I don't want to fight you."

His blue eyes were the color of a stormy sky. "If you don't, we need to work things out in a way that satisfies me."

Which meant she was going to have to share her baby with Noah, and not under one roof. Noah would take Ethan to the ranch and she wouldn't be with him. Was she making a giant mistake by not yielding to everything Noah wanted?

"Excuse me, Noah," she said, leaving the table and taking her dishes and wondering if the last few moments had been a turning point in their relationship and the harmony and compatibility were over.

She was loading her plate into the dishwasher when he came up behind her.

"I'll finish. You go do what you want," he said.

She turned to look at him. "What I want is to avoid fighting with you," she said, and they gazed at each other. After a moment he stepped close to put his arms around her.

"I don't like fighting, either. We have too much that's great between us. I want us together, Camilla, but we have to have certain things for a family to work, and we don't have those things at this point.

Let it go for now. Visit my ranch and see if that makes any difference for you."

She looked up at him and fought tears. "That's hard to do when you're talking about a lawyer," she whispered. "I think you expect me to make all the adjustments."

He stared at her. "I'll have to think about that one. I can tell you right now, Camilla, I'm not giving up being a rancher. I've worked in the company business and that life is not for me. I'm not a suit. I'm a cowboy and that's what I'm going to do." With that, he walked out of the kitchen, leaving her feeling as if she was heading straight for another heartbreak.

Could she deal with a male who was so strong-willed? Could she imagine life out on a ranch if Noah and Ethan were there? Was she making a disastrous mistake in not accepting Noah's way of life? She always came back to the same answer.

She didn't know.

Ten

Camilla

Two days later she was in a limo as they drove out to a waiting plane that belonged to Noah. She knew he had a pilot's license, but he wasn't flying today.

The plane was comfortable with plush seats and a big-screen television. Noah had some new toys for Ethan, who was happily playing with a stuffed tiger that roared. But most of her attention was on Noah. He was in tight jeans, a Western-style shirt and a Stetson, looking like the handsome rancher he was.

As her gaze ran over him again, she thought about their lovemaking in the early hours of the morning. The more they had sex, the more she wanted to. She was certain she was setting herself up for a terrible broken heart because she couldn't imagine working things out. He wouldn't change and she couldn't stop wanting her way. This visit to his ranch had pleased him enormously. He had been charming and sent her flowers again. But what she wanted was for Noah to make some concessions.

As she watched Noah play with Ethan, she felt another stab of pain because Noah was a great dad and it was too bad he'd be with his son only half the time. Ethan needed both of them.

She wouldn't let herself think about being married to Noah. She didn't think they would last together more than a few months and she'd already had a brief marriage. She thought about Aiden. She knew the first week she had made a mistake marrying him. She didn't want another marriage that crashed and burned in two short months.

Noah placed his hand on her wrist and she looked at him.

"We're about to fly over my ranch," he said.

She looked out the window, her gaze skimming the miles of mesquite and cacti below with an arroyo cutting through the earth in a jagged gash. And then they flew over another fence and the mesquite and cacti were gone, replaced by pasture, and she saw cattle by a large pond. They flew over more fences, and horses were scattered on more grassland. They flew over a stock tank. She saw a pickup driving on a dirt road, stirring a plume of dust, then more areas of mesquite, more cattle. She knew ranches were big, but Noah's was larger than she had envisioned.

"This is all your ranch?"

"All of it. Even beyond what you can see. We can circle it if you'd like."

She shook her head. "I'd rather get there. We might be pushing our luck with how good Ethan has been buckled into that seat."

Smiling, Noah nodded and turned his attention back to Ethan.

She took the opportunity to study Noah. The sight of his well-shaped hands made her remember how they felt on her skin. She drew a deep breath and looked up to meet his gaze.

His chest expanded as he drew a deep breath. "Save those thoughts and come back to them when we're home," he said in a husky voice.

She could feel her cheeks grow warm. "You're too dang perceptive," she said and turned to the window. Soon the pilot announced the landing, and as they came in, they flew over structures spread out in all directions. She felt as if she was looking at a small town of large impressive houses, of long barns, corrals and outbuildings.

Noah had put a map on her iPad and sent her a virtual tour of the house, so she had an idea what to expect, but seeing it in real life was different because his home, the grounds, the outbuildings, everything was far bigger, more lavish than she'd expected.

Her attention was caught by the views of a sprawling stacked stone mansion with porches, balconies off the second-floor rooms, slate roofs, a large pond in front of and around one side of the mansion with splashing fountains. Three statues of mountain lions were in well-tended flower beds in the front. And then the plane banked and she glimpsed a landing strip on his ranch. As they came in, she saw a waiting limo and a chauffeur in boots, jeans and a Western hat.

After introductions, they were driven around to a back entrance. As they circled the mansion that looked like a castle out on a windswept mesquite-covered flatland, she was surprised by the house. His condo in Dallas was beautiful and covered the entire top floor of a tall building owned by Noah, but this went beyond that, went beyond even his parents' home. Finding it in the middle of nowhere made it even more impressive.

The chauffeur held the door and Noah took Ethan, holding him easily. The chauffeur brought their things and a man came out the back door to greet them.

"Camilla, this is Terrance Holidaye, my house manager."

"Terrance, this is Ms. Warner, and this is my son, Ethan Warner."

"Ah, fine fellow. So happy to meet you, Ms. Warner."

"I'm glad to meet you," she said, smiling. "And thank you. We think Ethan is a fine fellow, too," she said, and they all smiled.

"Let me take that bag for you," Terrance said, taking a bag Camilla carried that held some of Ethan's things.

They crossed a porch that had hanging plants, pots of flowers and palm trees. Terrance held the door for them and they entered a wide entry hall with a splashing fountain, a two-story-high ceiling with an enormous crystal chandelier, paintings on the walls, benches upholstered in leather and a stone floor.

When they entered the kitchen, she was even more surprised because it was a huge room, with doors open to the back. She met Gilda Bascomb, his cook, a smiling, gray-haired woman. Enticing smells filled the kitchen as Gilda stirred something on the gas range.

When they walked back into the hall, Noah smiled at her. "Welcome to Bar G Ranch."

"Thank you. This mansion doesn't really reflect you."

"How so?" he asked, sounding amused.

"You're sort of laid-back and this is showy. It's spectacular, breathtaking, very impressive."

"Well, what do you know—I've impressed you," he said, looking more amused. "Now if I could just get you to like it, it would be worth the cost and the trouble."

"Noah, we don't have any commitment to one another," she reminded him, and again, that wall seemed to rise between them and his smile faded.

"No, we don't. We just have a baby." His voice was

cold and she knew she had dampened the moment, which she regretted, but it was the truth.

"You said you have a nursery ready and baby-proofed."

"Yes. It has furniture, but I'd like to leave the decorating to you if you would like to do it."

"Sure. I can do that," she said, wondering to what extent their lives would be interwoven.

"After you selected the furniture and I had it sent here, I contacted my house manager and told him I wanted the nursery and the family room baby-proofed. He has children, so I'm confident those rooms will be safe for Ethan."

"That's great, Noah."

"Mama," Ethan said, dropping his toy, holding out his arms and wiggling to get out of Noah's arms.

Camilla scooped up the toy, took Ethan and gave Noah the stuffed tiger.

"Here's the family room," he said, as they exited the kitchen into the hall and walked through wide double doors. The big room was two stories high with a beamed ceiling and polished dark wood walls, with one wall all glass. Another wall had floor-to-ceiling windows and large double doors with the upper half allowing a view of an outdoor living area with a large fire pit in the center and an outdoor kitchen. Off the patio was a fenced, lit, kidney-shaped swimming pool with palm trees at one end, and boulders and waterfalls and a fountain in the center. Cabanas to one side were partially hidden by flowers and palm trees.

"You have a palace here. How do you keep the palm trees from freezing?"

"There's a framework that isn't visible when it isn't used. It pulls a canopy over them and that's enough protection. Plus they're sheltered from the north wind by the house. I had the fence put in immediately after learning I'd have a baby here. Later, when he's older, I'll have a little kid pool built."

She turned to look at the family room again. "This is beautiful, Noah." She noticed a baby gate secured at the staircase to keep Ethan from climbing to the second floor that had a library circling the room. "It does look baby-proof." The tables were bare and the large fireplace had a bumper pad on the hearth. "Terrance did a good job."

"That's good to hear." Noah stood facing her and she realized he was watching her intently.

"What? I know I don't have food on my face."

"Just wondering if this is like your grandfather's house. You didn't like going there."

"There is nothing here to make me think of his ranch," she said, realizing Noah wanted her to see she had a mistaken view of ranches by thinking they would all be like her grandfather's. "Not even remotely. No, Noah, this will never remind me of my grandfather's ranch, which he didn't keep up. This is entirely different, except it is still far from the city."

"Ahh, the city," he said. "Your opera and shops and traffic and noise. We don't have that here," he said, reminding her of how opposite they were. He walked closer to place his hand lightly on her shoulder and twiddle with long locks of her hair. They were opposites in so many ways, but the physical attraction was mutual. "I'm glad you came to visit," he said, sounding sincere. "That means a lot, Camilla."

He leaned down to kiss her, a light kiss, but one that made her want to forget their differences and step into his arms.

"Dada, up."

She moved back and looked down at Ethan, who was holding Noah's leg.

Noah laughed and picked him up. "I don't think he wants me kissing Mama."

"I think he just wants to join in the hugs and kisses," she said, smiling at Ethan.

Taking Ethan when he reached for her, Camilla kissed his cheek and then looked at the room again. "This is a wonderful home, Noah."

"Inside that big closet, there should be a toy box—no lid—and some new toys, but let's go upstairs now and let me show you your suite, mine and the nursery. We can settle in, and when you want to, and Ethan is ready, I'll show you the rest of the house."

She smiled at him. "That ought to take about how many hours?"

"We can break it up," he said, pausing at the foot of the stairs. "Let me carry him up the stairs," he said, taking Ethan before she could protest.

"Why do you have this big a house on your ranch?"

she asked. "You don't have anything like this in Dallas."

"This is home. It's comfortable and exactly what I want. And I have the family out here at least once a month—or I did until I went into the Army. They haven't been out since I got discharged, but Stefanie told me they're coming soon."

She wondered if Mia would be on Noah's ranch, and she didn't like to think of him with someone else, but felt it would be her fault if he was.

"And I assume that all these people who work for you live on the ranch," she said.

"Not all of them. I furnish a house here for any employee who I feel will be here a long time." He led her down the second-floor corridor and stopped outside one of the rooms. "Here are Ethan's digs. Keep in mind his suite isn't finished yet."

"Do you mind if I hang one of my paintings in his room? I have three I've done for him that I haven't put up yet."

"I'd be glad to have your paintings."

They walked into a large playroom, and through an open door beyond it, she could see the crib.

"This suite has a bedroom, a playroom and a bathroom. And there's an adjoining suite where a nanny can stay."

He held Ethan with one arm and took her arm with his other hand. "Your suite is right next door and you have a connecting door to this room." He turned to her. "But I hope you're in my bed. We'll come back to that later when we've put the little one to bed," he said, and desire darkened his blue eyes. "I hired my cook to stay with Ethan when we go out tomorrow night. She has three little grandchildren, so she's been around babies, and she's worked for my family for twenty-two years. I hope that's all right with you."

"Yes, it is," she said, realizing from the moment she told Noah about Ethan, Ethan's life, as well as hers, had begun to change. He would be gone part of the time, influenced by Noah, would get to know and love his new family, who hovered over him more than hers did. She had known when she told Noah about Ethan there would be no going back. She just hoped there wouldn't be anything disastrous ahead.

"Now come see my suite," Noah said, leading her to cross the hall.

When they entered his suite, she saw a huge bedroom with floor-to-ceiling glass on one side that gave a panoramic view of his gardens and pools and lawn. He had a custom-made bed that was longer and wider than a king and covered in a dark blue comforter with a dozen pillows.

The floor was highly polished hardwood. Across from the bed was a huge TV. He had a glass-and-mahogany desk with two computers and four screens.

"Noah, you have a beautiful home."

He walked to her and placed his hands on her shoulders. "I hope you love it here. I'm glad you agreed to visit."

She looked up into blue eyes filled with desire.

With one hand, he lightly caressed her nape with feathery touches. She wanted his arms around her, wanted to kiss him. At the same time, she couldn't keep from thinking about her visit to the ranch. She had done what he wanted by agreeing to come. In addition, she'd had Ethan christened, specifically as a favor to Noah because of his father not being well, and she'd changed Noah's middle name. She had made all the moves, all the concessions so far, but not Noah. He was just like Thane and her dad. They were all nice men, but they just managed to believe that their worlds revolved around them and ran them the way they wanted.

She suspected this trip to the ranch—while definitely not what she'd expected—was only going to emphasize that, once again, she was dealing with a strong alpha male.

They spent the next hour getting familiar with the common living area of the house. They had lunch on the terrace with Ethan in his new high chair that she had bought in Dallas and Noah had shipped to the ranch. Later after Ethan's nap, they all got into a pickup, Ethan riding in the baby seat already installed in the back seat, and Noah drove them to one of the barns. He carried Ethan through the empty barn to a corral with horses. When one came to the fence, Ethan's eyes grew big as Noah let him pet the horse.

Camilla watched father and son and felt another clutch to her heart. Noah was so at ease on his ranch, so happy here. She had agreed to stay at least until

Wednesday and let Noah follow his regular routine on the weekdays so she could see what life was like. She knew he wanted her to like it the way he did.

Could she?

Noah

That evening they had a steak dinner that Noah cooked on the grill and they ate in the informal dining area off the kitchen that overlooked the patio and pool. Ethan was in his high chair between him and Camilla.

She looked relaxed and at ease in jeans and her hair in a ponytail. Noah wanted her to like the ranch. Until she'd said she was willing to visit, he'd felt they didn't have a future together. When he had come home from the service, he had never planned to get back with her, but the instant he knew about Ethan that had all changed. He wanted Ethan to have a mom and dad and he felt Camilla would be the best possible mom because Ethan was her own baby and it was obvious she loved him deeply.

Noah thought about their nights together. Her attraction for him hadn't diminished one degree since they'd been apart. She was still the sexiest woman he had known, irresistible in too many ways, and he had never really gotten over her. But he wasn't turning his life upside down, giving up being a rancher and moving to Dallas because that was what she liked best. Even if she liked the ranch, he was still too much the alpha male for her. That was something he couldn't change. If she couldn't adjust to it, there wasn't much he could do. So he took charge. So what? Would she prefer a guy who would stand back in a crisis and let the house burn down and him with it if no one else saved him?

Noah shook his head. And as far as he was concerned, Camilla was as strong-willed and decisive and as take-charge as he was. He had talked about this one time to her brother. He remembered Thane laughing and saying, *You two will always butt heads, but she can hold her own with you. She ought to see it in herself, but she doesn't. She couldn't be like our mom if she tried.*

He suspected Thane was absolutely right.

Now, his ranch was another matter. He might figure out something. Maybe spend some time in the city—he was there to see his family anyway—and get her to spend some time on his ranch. After all, she'd finally come to visit the Bar G. That was a big indication that she was trying to work things out because until recently, she wouldn't even consider visiting.

Then it hit him. She was his guest at the ranch. She'd had Ethan's middle name changed to Noah's dad's name. She'd had Ethan christened. Noah had done nothing to work out the problems between them. Maybe he did need to give in a little on the ranch and stay in Dallas. But before he made that move, he wanted to be sure of his feelings for her. From the first time he saw her again, he'd known he wasn't over her.

But before he could explore those feelings, he learned about Ethan and the baby changed everything.

Noah glanced at his desk, where he had the picture of Ethan she had given him. Ethan was a marvel and Noah already loved him deeply. How could a baby ensnare his heart so easily? Ethan didn't talk. He babbled and toddled around, but Noah loved him and thought he was adorable.

He knew the depth of his feelings for Ethan—it was boundless, unconditional love. How deep did his feelings run for Camilla? If he loved her, would he be thinking of getting a lawyer and, if necessary, initiating a custody suit? How much was he willing to sacrifice or change in his life to keep her? Could they ever work out their differences?

When she put Ethan to bed and tiptoed out of his room, Noah was waiting. He crossed the hall to wrap his arms around her.

"Noah, I want to sleep close to him."

"I have monitors that pick up every little sound. He'll be fine."

"Still, I would—" Noah kissed her and stopped her argument, and by the time he stopped kissing her, she didn't protest when he picked her up and carried her to his bedroom to make love.

Camilla

Noah took her and Ethan to show them the animals on Friday and he even took the baby for his first horse ride. Holding him, he rode slowly around the corral, going at a walk. Ethan looked delighted.

Finally late Friday afternoon Gilda drove from her ranch house to take charge of Ethan so Camilla would be free to dress. Camilla wondered about the evening ahead. She had gone dancing once before with Noah in Fort Worth and at the time it had been fun. Noah was the one who had taught her the two-step.

She dressed in a tight-fitting red knit shirt with a scoop neck, tight jeans, a wide hand-tooled leather belt and black boots. She wore a black Resistol, and let her hair fall loosely down her shoulders.

When she came downstairs, Noah crossed the hall to place his hands on her hips. "You look smokin' hot, darlin'."

She smiled. "I could say the same to you. I just kissed Ethan goodbye and he's happy with Gilda, so they seem to be doing all right."

"She's good with kids. I've seen her with her own grandkids and ranch kids. Let's go have some fun," he said, slipping his arm around her waist and walking toward the door to the portico where he had parked his pickup.

They drove to a small nearby roadhouse where music blared, neon lights flashed outside and the parking lot was filled with pickups. Inside, the music was loud, compliments of a drummer and two fiddlers. The scrape of boots on the floor was a constant swish as dancers circled.

When they reached a booth and slid into it, Camilla laughed. "You must know everyone in the next six counties. I'd guess it's taken us thirty minutes to get here from the door. I got some 'drop dead' looks from women, so you must be a popular guy out here."

He grinned. "I know what kind of looks you got from the guys. And you met about eight who work for me. They'll come ask you to dance."

A waitress in tight black slacks and a black T-shirt took their order and then Noah asked Camilla to dance.

During the evening as she circled the floor with him, she realized this was the most fun she'd had in a long time. Noah was filled with energy. He was happy, enjoying the night, and she was having fun with him.

It was almost midnight when he caught her around the waist and lifted her in the air as the music stopped. "Let's go home, okay?" Noah suggested, and she nodded.

He took her arm and in minutes they were in his pickup, headed back to his ranch. She threw her hat in the back and leaned against the seat, watching him drive. "Noah, that was fun. How often do you do that?"

"About once every month or two."

"You love this life, don't you?"

"Yes. If you'll visit me again or come to the ranch on a regular basis, I'll have a studio for you. Also, it's not as far from here to Taos and Santa Fe as it is from Dallas. I can open an art gallery in Santa Fe if you'd like. I don't know one thing about an art gallery, but you do. You could hire people to run it."

Startled, she shifted to face him as he drove. "I don't know. I'll have to think about coming here on a regular basis. I'm sure it would be a quiet, peaceful place to paint. I'll think about it," she said, watching him, reminded again that she was the one being asked to yield on some of their differences. So far, Noah still hadn't done one thing in that respect.

After a moment of silence, he spoke. "Camilla, thanks for deciding to come visit my ranch. That's a start on working things out between us. Ethan should have a mom and dad in his life, if we can work things out. That may not be possible, but coming to the ranch to visit is a start."

She gazed up at him and wondered if they were one bit closer now than before she told him she would visit his ranch. Maybe it would finally come down to whether Noah loved her or not, and so far, she didn't know. She wasn't going to declare her love when he never came close to saying he loved her.

Would she ever know the extent of Noah's feelings for her?

Eleven

Camilla

"I'm glad to be home," Noah said, unbuttoning his shirt. She turned to him, looking at the open vee of his shirt and his muscled chest with the thick black curls across it, and her mouth went dry.

"You look sexy tonight," he said, looking at her with desire filling his expression and making her pulse race. "You take my breath away and you have every time I've looked at you."

She caught his wrist. "Let's go to the bedroom now."

He picked her up and carried her easily, setting her on her feet by the big bed. He turned on one small lamp and then faced her, slowly peeling her out of her shirt and jeans. She held his shoulders while he pulled off her boots.

She stepped closer, her breasts just touching his chest while she disposed of her bra and panties. At the same time, he undressed. He was aroused, thick, hard and ready.

She leaned slightly closer and rubbed her bare breasts against his chest. He inhaled deeply and cupped her breasts in his hands. His hands were calloused, but his touch was gentle, light while his thumbs circled her nipples.

She gasped with pleasure and ran her hand over his chest, down over his flat, muscled belly. She knelt to stroke and fondle his hard rod, her other hand slipping between his legs to stroke him lightly. She ran her tongue over him and then took him in her mouth.

He inhaled, his hands tunneling in her hair while he let her caress and kiss him. With a groan, he pulled her to her feet to look into her eyes, a stormy, heated look of burning desire that sent a sizzling thrill over her.

"I want you," he whispered. He ran his hands slowly over her, caressing her breasts, down to her belly, down between her legs, rubbing her lightly. She gasped, closing her legs over his fingers as he stroked her and sensations rocked her, building in her until she grasped his arms and release shook her.

He kissed her hard, a demanding, possessive kiss filled with passion and desire and setting her ablaze again. She clung to him, rubbing against him, while his fingers played with her intimately, and within moments she was lost to sensation.

"I want you," she whispered, running her tongue over his ear.

He picked her up to carry her to bed, yanking away the covers and placing her on the bed while she watched him, wanting him, tingling from head to toe with longing for his hands and mouth on her again.

He rolled her over, getting above her and sliding his thick erection between her legs while he trailed kisses on her nape and reached beneath her to fondle her breasts.

With a moan, she rolled over, raising her legs to put them on either side of him.

Instead, he caught her ankles and put her legs on his shoulders, giving him access to her, to stroke and tease her. He ran his fingers over her and then his tongue.

"Noah, I want you," she whispered, clutching the bed, unable to reach him.

Sensations tantalized, built desire until suddenly he moved her legs to the bed and reached for a packet to put on a condom.

He entered her, thick and hard, moving slowly. Crying out, she arched and clutched his hard butt, pulling him toward her, wanting him in her to the hilt.

He eased back and she cried out again as he slowly filled her and withdrew. "Make this last. I want to love the night away," he whispered, entering her and withdrawing even more slowly, driving her to arch beneath him, to cry out for him.

He fought to keep control as long as he could, trying to pleasure her, to build the need, to make the moments sexier with each thrust. But he couldn't maintain his control any longer and he thrust into her, moving fast and then faster, pumping while she matched his moves and clung to him.

Rocking with him, she stiffened and arched against him as another blinding climax slammed into her. Dimly she heard him say her name and then she felt his own shuddering release.

He lowered his weight on her and they held each other, bound together in a rapturous union. She ran her hand lightly over his smooth, muscled back that was damp with sweat.

He turned to shower light kisses on her face and both of them were still breathing deeply.

Sometime later—she currently had no idea about time—he shifted and drew her into his arms, holding her. "You're fabulous," he whispered. "Better than I dreamed about."

She looked at his mouth while she slipped her hand behind his head and pulled him closer to kiss him.

"I want you in my arms all night." He held her close and they were quiet. She wondered if he was drifting off, but she didn't want to call his name and end the euphoria that enveloped her.

"Camilla," he said quietly. His voice was deep and

she looked at him as he held her close. "This is one thread that holds us together."

She looked in his eyes and had to agree. Being in bed with Noah was great, but not enough in the face of the issues separating them. She had visited the ranch and she would stay this week to see how daily life would be, but Noah was going to have to do some giving, too. She wasn't going to be the only one. Why couldn't he see what he needed to do?

He trailed his hand over the curve of her hip, and when he pulled her against him, she felt his manhood that was already hard again.

"You never stop," she whispered.

"You're the one who started this, just by being in my bed," he answered and kissed her. His fingers slipped between her thighs, and in no time she no longer cared who'd started it. She only knew she wanted to finish.

"I want you in me, loving me," she whispered, running her fingers lightly over him, more aware of his fingers playing between her thighs, another delicious torment that was driving her need to greater heights. He retrieved a condom and then moved over her. For one moment as he looked into her eyes, she felt wanted, but she knew that was an illusion. He wanted her now and she would take that. After they climaxed together, she fell back into his embrace.

She gasped for breath. "You really are insatiable."

"You make me want you. I've dreamed of you,

fantasized pleasuring you, wanted to kiss and touch you," he said.

His words made her tingle all over. But there were never words of love from him. Never a declaration. She felt a clutch to her insides, an ache, because if he wasn't in love, they could never work out sharing Ethan.

He tilted her chin up while he looked into her eyes. As she gazed into his face, she couldn't guess what he was thinking or feeling.

"I hope you like the ranch, Camilla. We're going to have to find some common ground to work out keeping Ethan."

His answer hurt and she felt that if she wanted a life with Noah, she would have to always do everything his way. She couldn't constantly be the one to yield. Even then, there were no words of love from him. Not even a hint.

Noah was tough and he would stand firm for what he wanted. Tonight might be a goodbye of sorts. Their lives would be intertwined because of sharing Ethan, but this closeness would vanish. And all because she was the only one in love. And that hurt.

They slept in each other's arms. Waking in the night, she held him tightly and asked herself the same questions again. So much with Noah was wonderful, but if he wasn't in love, she didn't see much hope for them getting together to raise Ethan. She loved Noah, but was her love enough to tie her life to a male who so far hadn't made an effort to agree to anything she wanted?

With a sigh she turned to place her hand on his chest. Instantly his hand closed over hers. Turning, he drew her against him and held her as if he really loved her, but she assumed he didn't and what he did feel might vanish in the next months.

Twelve

Camilla

The plane touched down in Dallas before sunrise on Thursday. She hadn't been able to sleep on the flight, too wrapped up in memories of her time at the ranch. They'd gone to church on Sunday, meeting locals and eating at a café with his friends and neighbors. Then the first two days of the week, Noah had been up and gone doing his ranching work by the time she got up and she'd had the days with Ethan. When Ethan had napped, she'd worked out in Noah's home gym. And each night they'd shared a bed, and some of the best sex Camilla had ever experienced.

They lay down for a quick nap when they got to her house, and when she woke, Noah's side of the bed was empty. She dressed quickly and went to find him. She located him in the kitchen cooking breakfast. Her gaze ran over his tight jeans and blue-and-red plaid shirt.

"We're matching," she said, pointing out her red shirt and jeans.

Smiling, he turned off the burner and glanced at her. "Ethan is still asleep. I want to talk to you and hopefully this will be a good time. Can you wait for breakfast?"

He looked somber and she felt chill bumps rise on her arms. She had a feeling he had made some decisions, and dread filled her because his jovial manner was gone.

"Let's go into the family room," she said. "We'll hear him on the monitor."

Noah brought in two cups of coffee and set one beside her on a table.

He sat facing her in a brown leather wingback chair. He had one foot up on his other knee and watched her closely. "I wanted to talk while Ethan is asleep because we'll have fewer interruptions."

He sipped his coffee, she suspected more as a delay tactic than because he really wanted it. He put the cup down and met her eyes. "Listen, Camilla, we both know what this is about. We both need to think about what we want to do in our future. It's been wonderful to be with both you and Ethan. In a way I want to just keep on like we are now, but we know we have to make some decisions. We could go on this way for a lot longer, but eventually a time will come when we'll need to decide our future, and I think it's time now."

His words sent a shiver through her. She had known this was coming, but it hurt to hear it.

Not waiting for her reply, he continued. "I know how to take care of Ethan now and I have resources and a family who want him every second I'll let them have with him. You and I have talked about the future, but really haven't settled anything. I've told you what I want—a real family, a family that is together. A family where each member feels love and commitment. I don't want a long-distance relationship and I can't quit ranching and work in an office. That may be selfish, but there it is."

"So where do we go from here, Noah?" She had no answer because the answer she wanted to hear wouldn't happen. She wanted them to stay together. She wanted Noah to be in love with her, to love her the way she did him. And she did love him. She would always love him. But Noah couldn't feel that way about her or he wouldn't have said what he just did. He wouldn't want to move out and leave her. If he loved her, he would stay. She fought back tears because she was terrified of what Noah would suggest for Ethan.

"Listen to me," Noah said, leaning forward, gazing into her eyes. "I want to work things out, Camilla. We have some great things going for us. The sex couldn't be better. We both adore Ethan. We both want to be a family for him. We are his parents and I want us together with him," he said, looking directly into her eyes.

Her heart jumped when he said they both adored Ethan and they both wanted to be a family for him. The words gave her hope.

"If we can't work this out, then I want custody half the time."

Like a popped balloon, her optimism fizzled. She felt like she couldn't draw in oxygen. "Noah, we've been doing well together. Surely we can work this out."

"Before we get to a protracted court custody battle and there's no chance of turning back and feelings are hurt, why don't we try something? Let's have a trial run. I'll take Ethan for a week and then you take him for a week. Let's do that for a month and then see how we feel about things before we get lawyers involved," he suggested.

"I knew this was coming, but that doesn't stop it from hurting," she said and covered her eyes. "I'm sorry, Noah. I've never been away from him except for a night or two when he was with your folks. I can't imagine…" She let the unspoken words float between them as she took out a handkerchief and wiped her eyes.

He walked over to her to place his hands on her shoulders. "Camilla, we have never talked about love. I've skirted that the whole time I've been here and so have you. Neither of us has ever said 'I love you' to the other."

Her heart pounded and she wondered what was coming. A declaration of love? Reasons why he couldn't say it?

He gave her neither. "I'm still exploring my feelings," he said. "All the years in the military, I tried to get over what I felt for you. Now, since knowing about Ethan, I haven't really explored my feelings or let go because I felt like I would get hurt. You've never said 'I love you.'"

"You haven't either, Noah. It's hard to say 'I love you' when the other person doesn't say it. That's awkward." She was tempted to tell him now, though, before he walked out of her life.

"To be honest, Camilla, I've tried to keep from falling in love because I felt like it was inevitable that we would part. I still live and work on a ranch and I'm still the kind of man you dislike and we're still opposites in a ton of ways. When I marry, I want it to last. I want forever. I want what my family has. I can't marry and love a woman unless I can have that kind of love with her."

She stood to face him and placed her hands on his arms. "I don't know if we can ever work things out. You haven't made any effort to change except to move in with me to get to know Ethan and how to take care of him."

She had listened to him, hurting when he said he didn't know what he felt, hurting even more at the thought of giving up Ethan for a week. She'd known this would happen, but they had so many happy moments together she'd begun to hope for more. And they had made love constantly, something merely physical and lusty to Noah, but something emotional and honest for her. Each time they made love, it reinforced the love she had for him and made her hurt more than ever. If he didn't declare his love for her, did she want to tell him she loved him? Noah could view sex as sex. She couldn't. Sex was all tied up with love and intimacy. He hadn't made promises and hadn't declared love, but she'd still lost her heart to him long ago. She'd loved him the night she got pregnant. The only decision now was whether to tell him.

"Are you willing to try a week on and a week off for the next month?" he asked her.

"I don't see that I have much choice here, but that's better than getting lawyers involved. Noah, you told me you don't know the depth of your feelings. I don't know the depth of mine, because there are some things, like moving to your ranch, I don't think I could do, not for the whole year. But I do know that I love you. I've loved you for a long time and I missed you and cried over you while you were away in the Army."

He frowned and stepped closer. "Camilla—"

She held her hand up for him to stop. "You don't need to say anything now. Just tell me—when are you moving out?"

"I hadn't thought that through, but probably today. I'll pick Ethan up this weekend and start my week."

"It'll be a huge change to lose both of you at once.

Let me start with Ethan this week and you take him the following week. Will you do that?"

He nodded. "All right. I'll move out today. I'll get my things. Camilla—"

"Let's give this a try. I told you I love you. I don't want you to make any declaration or say anything in response to that until you've given it more thought. I want you to be sure of what you tell me."

He nodded. "I'll do that. I'll skip breakfast and get my things together and we'll get this done. One thing I'm very sure about is how much I'm going to miss both of you. But if we get together, I'd want you on my ranch year-round. I don't want a part-time wife or a part-time family."

She nodded and could feel tears on her cheeks. "I understand. That's why I went ahead and told you what I feel. I didn't think it'd make any difference."

He walked out of the room and she felt sure he was walking out of her life. They would see each other and interact because of Ethan, but a more intimate relationship with him was over forever.

That knowledge, together with the fact that she would have Ethan only half the time, hurt terribly, and she sat in the chair, putting her hands over her face while she cried.

Noah

Noah had his things gathered up and in his car before Ethan woke up. When he heard his son rouse, he went to the nursery. Camilla was already there, picking him up. She turned and saw Noah.

His heart felt as if a fist squeezed it. She had been crying and for once Ethan looked solemn. He held out his arms to Noah. "Dada," he said. "Up."

"May I have him? I'd like to hold him a few minutes before I leave."

"Of course," she said, handing her baby to Noah. Her hands were like ice and he felt bad about hurting her and he was still surprised by her firm declaration of love. He hadn't thought she was in love, real, serious love, and it had shocked him to hear her say that.

He held Ethan, looking at him, knowing he was going to miss him. Was he making a mistake by not telling her he loved her and proposing so they could all stay together? But he couldn't. He had to be sure of his feelings. He didn't want a marriage that would end in a few years.

"Ethan, I will miss you," he said, hurting and wondering if he was bringing all sorts of heartache on himself. Yet if he stayed months longer and then had to leave, it would be even more difficult.

He handed Ethan back to her and put his arm around her. "I'll miss you, too, Camilla. I'm headed for the ranch, but you can always get me by phone."

"Goodbye," she whispered and turned away. "Let yourself out, Noah."

He knew she was crying and he felt terrible as he walked out of the room and the house. He was flying back to the ranch later and he planned on working hard until late tonight. It was his way of getting over telling her goodbye.

First, though, he would go by his folks' house and break the news to them. He'd already sent a text to his siblings. All of them would miss Ethan, but when it was his week, he would take Ethan to see their parents and they could all go there to be with Ethan.

Camilla

Camilla was sure Ethan picked up on her heartache and that was why he'd lost some of his smiles. She finally sat on the floor to play with him, but after a few minutes, she looked at his black curly hair, thought of Noah and started crying again, causing Ethan to cry.

"We miss him, don't we?" she asked her baby.

"Mama," he said and patted her knee.

She hugged him and cried, missing Noah, hurting because she loved him. Could she possibly stand living on that ranch year-round? She had always said she wouldn't leave the city. Part of the year wouldn't be so bad, but year-round? How much could she live there?

She shook her head. He hadn't asked her to move there and he hadn't proposed or said he loved her. In fact, he had admitted he didn't know what he felt.

"I miss your daddy," she told Ethan, and he gazed solemnly at her. He held out his arms.

"Up," he said, and she pulled him close to hug him.

She spent the day playing with him. She postponed painting, an appointment, shopping for new clothes for

Ethan. She could do all that the next week when Noah had him. Right now, she just wanted to be with him, hold him, read to him and play with him. She missed Noah more as the hours of the morning passed. How long was she going to miss him this badly? She didn't think she would ever get over him.

Noah

Friday, a week later, Noah drove his pickup back to the ranch house from the pasture. He was dusty from moving cattle from one pasture to another with a bunch of cowboys. He got a cold beer and sat on the patio, looking at his pool before he went up to shower. He wasn't sleeping nights and it hurt far more than he expected to be away from Camilla and Ethan. It hurt far worse than it had when he had broken up with her and gone into the Army. He missed his son. He missed Camilla, especially at night. She had visited the ranch, stayed longer than originally planned. She had been more cooperative than he had been actually, he realized. He spent all sorts of time in Dallas. Couldn't he live with a wife who visited the city some?

He heard a car and saw a red sports car whip around and park at the back gate.

He smiled. Stef. He'd be glad to see her.

She jumped out and slammed the door, rushing through the gate, and he wondered what was up because she was charging toward the porch. He stood up and waited until she was close and he held up his beer. "Want a cold one?"

She rushed in front of him and stood with her hands on her hips. "No, I don't. You're a miserable louse."

He had to laugh. "Hello to you, too. What bee got into your bonnet?"

"It isn't funny, Noah."

He realized she actually was mad at him, something that had rarely happened since they'd been teenagers. "What the hell, Stef? I've been out here working my tail off. What did I do?"

"You moved out and left Camilla and Ethan."

His smile vanished. "We didn't have anything permanent. We're doing a trial run of alternating weeks with Ethan. We'd planned to do this all along. I just moved in with her to get to know Ethan and to learn how to take care of him. You knew that. Sit down and we'll talk."

Instead, she held her ground. "I went over to see her and she couldn't talk to me without getting tears in her eyes. And I miss Ethan."

"Stef, butt out. I don't want to rush into marriage. And Camilla's already had one divorce."

"Well, yeah, she married on the rebound because she was hurting over you and she was already pregnant."

"Did she tell you all that?"

"We got to be close friends. Actually, we're sort of related now because of Ethan."

"Stef, this isn't any of your business."

"You don't say. It will affect our whole family." She stared at him. "So how are you getting along out here?"

"Don't start in on me. I miss them. I knew I would."

"Do you really? You seemed real happy when you were with them. Are you real happy out here now?"

He sighed deeply. "Do you know this is absolutely none of your business?"

"Are you really happy?" she asked, sounding sincere. "I'm worried about you."

"I'm okay, and no, I'm not so happy. She won't marry me and live out here year-round."

"Sometimes you can be annoyingly stubborn. That's simple to fix. Come to Dallas some of the time. You think you're not coming to see us? You spend plenty of time there. Noah, you're hurting yourself. You're hurting Camilla, and worst of all, you're hurting Ethan."

"You can't tell me he misses me. He's a little baby and they adjust."

"He needs his daddy and you know it. You're unhappy and it's all your own fault. You'll just have him half of the time. He needs both of you all of the time. I love you and I'm worried about all three of you. It's you causing the trouble and hurting yourself. She said you don't love her."

"I don't know what I feel."

"You're smarter than that. I'll tell you what. If you

don't know what you feel, I think you're in for some rough times. Unfortunately, you cause others to hurt."

She got ready to leave. "I've had my say. Now I'll drive back to the city, and I'm going to tell Camilla you're not happy either and then I'm going to play with your son. I'll ask her out with my crowd Saturday night and see if that will cheer her up a little. Ben and Hallie will keep Ethan."

"Now you're interfering."

"No, I'm not. You moved out. She's free as a bird. I hate to see you hurt yourself and keep yourself from happiness. You're just being plain stubborn, Noah." She looked around at the ranch. "This is nice, Noah, but it's just a house. It doesn't mean anything by itself. Now, I know you could be happy out here in a shack, but the ranch is just mesquite, cattle and horses. If you want that more…" She threw up her hands. "I miss Ethan and I'm going back to Dallas to play with him. 'Bye, Noah." She left as fast as she came and in seconds the red sports car roared away.

Noah stood looking at his ranch, thinking about Ethan and Camilla. Stefanie had been right about everything. He would spend time in Dallas with his family. He had good people working for him who could manage the ranch just fine in his absence. His wife didn't have to stay year-round on his ranch.

He was definitely unhappy at the moment. He missed them both. The big question was: Did he love Camilla?

Thirteen

Camilla

Camilla stood pushing Ethan in the swing. Noah called and said he wanted to come talk and she couldn't keep from hoping it was something good and that he wasn't coming to tell her about seeing his attorney. She knew it was probably wishful thinking but she couldn't help it.

Stefanie called too and asked if she could come get Ethan. Her folks wanted to see him and she did, too.

Camilla thought about Noah coming. He would want to see his son, but he could go on to his folks' house, which he probably planned to do anyway, so she told Stefanie to come get him.

She heard a car and saw Stefanie drive up, so she

got Ethan out of the swing and picked up the bag she was sending with him.

In minutes he was buckled in Stefanie's car and she was gone with a wave. Camilla was happy for the family to have Ethan, but when Noah took him for his week, it was going to hurt badly. Would she ever get accustomed to kissing him goodbye and being without him?

She walked back to the house and heard the second car and saw it was Noah. He stepped out and her heart thudded. It took an effort not to run and hug him. He looked incredible, tall, handsome, filled with energy that showed in his walk. He had on jeans and boots and a blue cotton Western-style shirt and his black hat.

She had missed him more than when he'd left for the Army. If he started talking about sharing Ethan, she hoped she could hold back the tears this time.

As he came closer, she was aware of her own clothes—cutoffs, a navy knit shirt and sneakers.

"Hi. You just missed Stefanie picking up Ethan. He's at your folks' house if you want to go see him when you—"

Noah didn't stop. He walked up, wrapped his arms around her and kissed away her words.

Her heart thudded and she clung to him tightly with her arms around his narrow waist. Still kissing her, he picked her up and carried her into her house, not putting her down till he reached the family room.

He tossed his hat to a chair. "I've missed you."

Her heart began to pound. He hadn't kissed like he was going to talk about attorneys and taking Ethan half the time.

"We've missed you. Ethan looks for you. I know he's missing you, so I hope you have time to go see him."

"Camilla, I've got something to say and I don't want to waste one more minute to say it. I want to see if we can work out something where I'll be on the ranch part of the time and we'll be in Dallas part of the time." He took her hand. "I love you. I thought about my feelings for you and they run deep. I missed you the whole time I was in the Army. I kept thinking I was getting over you because I didn't see you, but the minute I saw you when I came home, I knew I wasn't over you at all."

"Oh, Noah, I love you. I have for so long—way before you went into the Army." She threw her arms around his neck and kissed him.

When he raised his head to look at her, he still held her tightly in his arms. "I can come to Dallas—I always have. Are you willing to spend a lot of time on the ranch? I'll spend a lot of time in Dallas."

Laughing with joy, she nodded. "Yes. Oh, yes. We'll be a family, Noah. We'll be together."

He reached into his pocket. "Camilla, will you marry me?"

Joy burst in her and she tightened her arms around him, standing on tiptoe to kiss him. He held her tightly while they kissed and then she leaned away. "Yes.

Yes, yes, yes, I'll marry you. Today if you want. Oh, Noah, I love you and have loved you for so long. I've been miserable without you."

He released her and took her hand. "I love you and want to marry you." He opened his hand to put a small box in her hand.

She looked at it and then opened it to find another fancy box inside. She opened it and gasped. "Oh, my! That is the most gorgeous ring ever!" she said, looking at a huge diamond with smaller diamonds around it.

He took it from her to slip it on her finger. "If it doesn't fit we can take it to the jeweler."

"It fits. It's magnificent. My, oh, my."

"It is only a symbol of what I feel. I love you," he said. "Come on. I want to go get Ethan and you can show the family and tell them."

"Should we have a wedding date? They'll ask."

He shook his head. "Let's do that later. I want them to know and I want to see Ethan." He hesitated a moment. "Maybe we should let him stay with them tonight. We have some catching up to do in the bedroom."

She wrapped her arms around his neck again, looking at her ring sparkle before she turned to him. "You've made me the happiest woman in Texas today!"

He laughed and hugged her. "I'm definitely the happiest man," he said as he kissed away her answer.

* * * * *

*If you liked this story of an alpha hero tamed
by love—and a baby—
don't miss the next*
BILLIONAIRES AND BABIES *story*

HEART OF A TEXAN

By USA TODAY *bestselling author
Charlene Sands
Available September 2018!*

Or any of these other
BILLIONAIRES AND BABIES *stories:*

*HIS ACCIDENTAL HEIR by Joanne Rock
THE CEO'S NANNY AFFAIR by Joss Wood
THE CHRISTMAS BABY BONUS
by* USA TODAY *bestselling author Yvonne Lindsay
TAMING THE TEXAN by Jules Bennett*

***

*If you're on Twitter, tell us what you think
of Harlequin Desire! #harlequindesire*

From New York Times *bestselling author
Maisey Yates comes the sizzling second book in her
new* GOLD VALLEY *Western romance
series. Shy tomboy Kaylee Capshaw never thought
she'd have a chance of winning the heart of her
longtime friend Bennett Dodge, even if he is the
cowboy of her dreams.*

*But when she learns he's suddenly single, can she
finally prove to him that the woman he's been
waiting for has been right here all along?*

*Read on for a sneak peek at
UNTAMED COWBOY,
the latest in* New York Times
bestselling author Maisey Yates's
GOLD VALLEY *series!*

CHAPTER ONE

KAYLEE CAPSHAW NEEDED a new life. Which was why she was steadfastly avoiding the sound of her phone vibrating in her purse while the man across from her at the beautifully appointed dinner table continued to talk, oblivious to the internal war raging inside of her.

Do not look at your phone.

The stern internal admonishment didn't help. Everything in her was still seized up with adrenaline and anxiety over the fact that she had texts she wasn't looking at.

Not because of her job. Any and all veterinary emergencies were being covered by her new assistant at the clinic, Laura, so that she could have this date with Michael, the perfectly nice man she was now ignoring while she warred within herself to *not look down at her phone.*

No. It wasn't work texts she was itching to look at.

But what if it was Bennett?

Laura knew that she wasn't supposed to interrupt

Kaylee tonight, because Kaylee was on a date, but she had conveniently not told Bennett. Because she didn't want to talk to Bennett about her dating anyone.

Mostly because she didn't want to hear if Bennett was dating anyone. If the woman lasted, Kaylee would inevitably know all about her. So there was no reason—in her mind—to rush into all of that.

She wasn't going to look at her phone.

"Going over the statistical data for the last quarter was really very interesting. It's fascinating how the holidays inform consumers."

Kaylee blinked. "What?"

"Sorry. I'm probably boring you. The corporate side of retail at Christmas is probably only interesting to people who work in the industry."

"Not at all," she said. Except, she wasn't interested. But she was trying to be. "How exactly did you get involved in this job living here?"

"Well, I can do most of it online. Sometimes I travel to Portland, which is where the corporate office is." Michael worked for a world-famous brand of sports gear, and he did something with the sales. Or data.

Her immediate attraction to him had been his dachshund, Clarence, whom she had seen for a tooth abscess a couple of weeks earlier. Then on a follow-up visit he had asked if Kaylee would like to go out, and she had honestly not been able to think of one good reason she shouldn't. Except for Bennett Dodge. Her best friend since junior high and the obsessive focus of her hormones since she'd discovered what men and women did together in the dark.

Which meant she absolutely needed to go out with Michael.

Bennett couldn't be the excuse. Not anymore.

She had fallen into a terrible rut over the last couple of years while she and Bennett had gotten their clinic up and running. Work and her social life revolved around him. Social gatherings were all linked to him and to his family.

She'd lived in Gold Valley since junior high, and the friendships she'd made here had mostly faded since then. Shc'd made friends when she'd gone to school for veterinary medicine, but she and Bennett had gone together, and those friends were mostly mutual friends.

If they ever came to town for a visit, it included Bennett. If she took a trip to visit them, it often included Bennett.

The man was up in absolutely everything, and the effects of it had been magnified recently as her world had narrowed thanks to their mutually demanding work schedule.

That amount of intense, focused time with him never failed to put her in a somewhat pathetic emotional space.

Hence the very necessary date.

Then her phone started vibrating because it was ringing, and she couldn't ignore that. "I'm sorry," she said. "Excuse me."

It was Bennett. Her heart slammed into her throat.
She should not answer it. She really shouldn't. She
thought that even while she was pressing the green
accept button.

"What's up?" she asked.

"Calving drama. I have a breech one. I need some
help."

Bennett sounded clipped and stressed. And he
didn't stress easily. He delivered countless calves over
the course of the season, but a breech birth was never
good. If the rancher didn't call him in time, there was
rarely anything that could be done.

And if Bennett needed some assistance, then the
situation was probably pretty extreme.

"Where are you?" she asked, darting a quick look
over to Michael and feeling like a terrible human for
being marginally relieved by this interruption.

"Out of town at Dave Miller's place. Follow the
driveway out back behind the house."

"See you soon." She hung up the phone and looked
down at her half-finished dinner. "I am so sorry,"
she said, forcing herself to look at Michael's face.
"There's a veterinary emergency. I have to go."

She stood up, collecting her purse and her jacket.
"I really am sorry. I tried to cover everything. But
my partner… It's a barnyard thing. He needs help."

Michael looked… Well, he looked understanding.
And Kaylee almost wished that he wouldn't. That he
would be mad so that she would have an excuse to
storm off and never have dinner with him again. That

he would be unreasonable in some fashion so that she could call the date experiment a loss and go back to making no attempts at a romantic life whatsoever.

But he didn't. "Of course," he said. "You can't let something happen to an animal just because you're on a dinner date."

"I really can't," she said. "I'm sorry."

She reached into her purse and pulled out a twenty-dollar bill. She put it on the table and offered an apologetic smile before turning and leaving. Before he didn't accept her contribution to the dinner.

She was not going to make him pay for the entire meal on top of everything.

"Have a good evening," the hostess said as Kaylee walked toward the front door of the restaurant. "Please dine with us again soon."

Kaylee muttered something and headed outside, stumbling a little bit when her kitten heel caught in a crack in the sidewalk. That was the highest heel she ever wore, since she was nearly six feet tall in flats, and towering over one's date was not the best first impression.

But she was used to cowgirl boots and not these spindly, fiddly things that hung up on every imperfection. They were impractical. How any woman walked around in stilettos was beyond her.

The breeze kicked up, reminding her that March could not be counted on for warm spring weather as the wind stung her bare legs. The cost of wearing a dress. Which also had her feeling pretty stupid right about now.

She always felt weird in dresses, owing that to her stick figure and excessive height. She'd had to be tough from an early age. With parents who ultimately ended up ignoring her existence, she'd had to be self-sufficient.

It had suited her to be a tomboy because spending time outdoors, running around barefoot and climbing trees, far away from the fight scenes her parents continually staged in their house, was better than sitting at home.

Better to pretend she didn't like lace and frills, since her bedroom consisted of a twin mattress on the floor and a threadbare afghan.

She'd had a friend when she was little, way before they'd moved to Gold Valley, who'd had the prettiest princess room on earth. Lace bedding, a canopy. Pink walls with flower stencils. She'd been so envious of it. She'd felt nearly sick with it.

But she'd just said she hated girlie things. And never invited that friend over ever.

And hey, she'd been built for it. Broad shoulders and stuff.

Sadly, she *wasn't* built for pretty dresses.

But she needed strength more, anyway.

She was thankful she had driven her own truck, which was parked not far down the street against the curb. First-date rule for her. Drive your own vehicle. In case you had to make a hasty getaway.

And apparently she had needed to make a hasty getaway, just not because Michael was a weirdo or anything.

No, he had been distressingly nice.

She mused on that as she got into the driver's seat and started the engine. She pulled away from the curb and headed out of town. Yes, he had been perfectly nice. Really, there had been nothing wrong with him. And she was a professional at finding things wrong with the men she went on dates with. A professional at finding excuses for why a second date couldn't possibly happen.

She was ashamed to realize now that she was hoping he would consider this an excuse not to make a second date with her.

That she had taken a phone call in the middle of dinner and then had run off.

A lot of people had trouble dating. But often it was for deep reasons they had trouble identifying.

Kaylee knew exactly why she had trouble dating.

It was because she was in love with her best friend, Bennett Dodge. And he was *not* in love with her.

She gritted her teeth.

She wasn't in love with Bennett. No. She wouldn't allow that. She had lustful feelings for Bennett, and she cared deeply about him. But she wasn't in love with him. She refused to let it be that. Not anymore.

That thought carried her over the gravel drive that led to the ranch, back behind the house, just as Bennett had instructed. The doors to the barn were flung open, the lights on inside, and she recognized Bennett's truck parked right outside.

She killed the engine and got out, then moved into the barn as quickly as possible.

"What's going on?" she asked.

Dave Miller was there, his arms crossed over his chest, standing back against the wall. Bennett had his hand on the cow's back. He turned to look at her, the overhead light in the barn seeming to shine a halo around his cowboy hat. That chiseled face that she knew so well but never failed to make her stomach go tight. He stroked the cow, his large, capable hands drawing her attention, as well as the muscles in his forearm. He was wearing a tight T-shirt that showed off the play of those muscles to perfection. His large biceps and the scars on his skin from various on-the-job injuries. He had a stethoscope draped over his shoulders, and something about that combination—rough-and-ready cowboy meshed with concerned veterinarian—was her very particular catnip.

"I need to get the calf out as quickly as possible, and I need to do it at the right moment. Too quickly and we're likely to crush the baby's ribs." She had a feeling he said that part for the benefit of the nervous-looking rancher standing off to the side.

Dave Miller was relatively new to town, having moved up from California a couple of years ago with fantasies of rural living. A small ranch for him and his wife's retirement had grown to a medium-sized one over the past year or so. And while the older man had a reputation for taking great care of his animals, he wasn't experienced at this.

"Where do you want me?" she asked, moving over to where Bennett was standing.

"I'm going to need you to suction the hell out of this thing as soon as I get her out." He appraised her. "Where were you?"

"It doesn't matter."

"You're wearing a dress."

She shrugged. "I wasn't at home."

He frowned. "Were you out?"

This was not the time for Bennett to go overly concerned big brother on her. It wasn't charming on a normal day, but it was even less charming when she'd just abandoned her date to help deliver a calf. "If I wasn't at home, I was out. Better put your hand up the cow, Bennett," she said, feeling testy.

Bennett did just that, checking to see that the cow was dilated enough for him to extract the calf. Delivering a breech animal like this was tricky business. They were going to have to pull the baby out, likely with the aid of a chain or a winch, but not *too* soon, which would injure the mother. And not too quickly, which would injure them both.

But if they went too slow, the baby cow would end up completely cut off from its oxygen supply. If that happened, it was likely to never recover.

"Ready," he said. "I need chains."

She looked around and saw the chains lying on the ground, then she picked them up and handed them

over. He grunted and pulled, producing the first hint
of the calf's hooves. Then he lashed the chain around
them. He began to pull again, his muscles straining
against the fabric of his black T-shirt, flexing as he
tugged hard.

She had been a vet long enough that she was in-
ured to things like this, from a gross-out-factor per-
spective. But still, checking out a guy in the midst
of all of this was probably a little imbalanced. Of
course, that was the nature of how things were with
her and Bennett.

They'd met when she'd moved to Gold Valley at
thirteen—all long limbs, anger and adolescent awk-
wardness. And somehow, they'd fit. He'd lost his
mother when he was young, and his family was limp-
ing along. Her own home life was hard, and she'd
been desperate for escape from her parents' neglect
and drunken rages at each other.

She never had him over. She didn't want to be at
her house. She never wanted him, or any other friend,
to see the way her family lived.

To see her sad mattress on the floor and her peeling nightstand.

Instead, they'd spent time at the Dodge ranch. His
family had become hers, in many ways. They weren't
perfect, but there was more love in their broken pieces
than Kaylee's home had ever had.

He'd taught her to ride horses, let her play with
the barn cats and the dogs that lived on the ranch.
Together, the two of them had saved a baby squir-

rel that had been thrown out of his nest, nursing him back to health slowly in a little shoebox.

She'd blossomed because of him. Had discovered her love of animals. And had discovered she had the power to fix some of the broken things in the world.

The two of them had decided to become veterinarians together after they'd successfully saved the squirrel. And Bennett had never wavered.

He was a constant. A sure and steady port in the storm of life.

And when her feelings for him had started to shift and turn into more, she'd done her best to push them down because he was her whole world, and she didn't want to risk that by introducing anything as volatile as romance.

She'd seen how that went. Her parents' marriage was a reminder of just how badly all that could sour. It wasn't enough to make her swear off men, but it was enough to make her want to keep her relationship with Bennett as it was.

But that didn't stop the attraction.

If it were as simple as deciding not to want him, she would have done it a long time ago. And if it were as simple as being with another man, that would have worked back in high school when she had committed to finding herself a prom date and losing her virginity so she could get over Bennett Dodge already.

It had not worked. And the sex had been disappointing.

So here she was, fixating on his muscles while he helped an animal give birth.

Maybe there wasn't a direct line between those two things, but sometimes it felt like it. If all other men could just...not be so disappointing in comparison to Bennett Dodge, things would be much easier.

She looked away from him, making herself useful, gathering syringes and anything she would need to clear the calf of mucus that might be blocking its airway. Bennett hadn't said anything, likely for Dave's benefit, but she had a feeling he was worried about the health of the heifer. That was why he needed her to see to the calf as quickly as possible, because he was afraid he would be giving treatment to its mother.

She spread a blanket out that was balled up and stuffed in the corner—unnecessary, but it was something to do. Bennett strained and gave one final pull and brought the calf down as gently as possible onto the barn floor.

"There he is," Bennett said, breathing heavily. "There he is."

His voice was filled with that rush of adrenaline that always came when they worked jobs like this.

She and Bennett ran the practice together, but she typically held down the fort at the clinic and treated smaller domestic animals like birds, dogs, cats and the occasional ferret.

Bennett worked with large animals, cows, horses, goats and sometimes llamas. They had a mobile unit for things like this.

But when push came to shove, they helped each other out.

And when push came to pulling a calf out of its mother, they definitely helped each other.

Bennett took care of the cord and then turned his focus back to the mother.

Kaylee moved to the calf, who was glassy-eyed and not looking very good. But she knew from her limited experience with this kind of delivery that just because they came out like this didn't mean they wouldn't pull through.

She checked his airway, brushing away any remaining mucus that was in the way. She put her hand back over his midsection and tried to get a feel on his heartbeat. "Bennett," she said, "stethoscope?"

"Here," he said, taking it from around his neck and tossing it her direction. She caught it and slipped the ear tips in, then pressed the diaphragm against the calf, trying to get a sense of what was happening in there.

His heartbeat sounded strong, which gave her hope.

His breathing was still weak. She looked around at the various tools, trying to see something she might be able to use. "Dave," she said to the man standing back against the wall. "I need a straw."

"A straw?"

"Yes. I've never tried this before, but I hear it works."

She had read that sticking a straw up a calf's nose

irritated the system enough that it jolted them into breathing. And she hoped that was the case.

Dave returned quickly with the item that she had requested, and Kaylee moved the straw into position. Not gently, since that would defeat the purpose.

You had to love animals to be in her line of work. And unfortunately, loving them sometimes meant hurting them.

The calf startled, then heaved, his chest rising and falling deeply before he started to breathe quickly.

Kaylee pulled the straw out and lifted her hands. "Thank God."

Bennett turned around, shifting his focus to the calf and away from the mother. "Breathing?"

"Breathing."

He nodded, wiping his forearm over his forehead. "Good." His chest pitched upward sharply. "I think Mom is going to be okay, too."

UNTAMED COWBOY
by New York Times *bestselling author*
Maisey Yates,
available July 2018 wherever
HQN Books and ebooks are sold.
www.Harlequin.com

#2605 HEART OF A TEXAN

Billionaires and Babies • by Charlene Sands

To protect her baby daughter, runaway heiress Francesca has fled home...only to find herself hired on at a Texas billionaire's ranch! But as the secrets—and desire—build between them, she'll soon have to reveal who she really is...

#2606 LONE STAR SECRETS

Texas Cattleman's Club: The Impostor • by Cat Schield

Fashion mogul Megan was at her husband's funeral when the man she thought she'd married walked into the ceremony. As an impostor's scheme to impersonate his billionaire best friend unravels, will she have a second chance with her real husband?

#2607 A SNOWBOUND SCANDAL

Dallas Billionaires Club • by Jessica Lemmon

Wealthy Texas politician Chase Ferguson ended things with his ex to protect her. Yet now she's crashed his isolated vacation house in a snowstorm. And when a stormbound seduction has real-world repercussions, he must make a stand for what—and who—he truly believes in.

#2608 WILD WYOMING NIGHTS

The McNeill Magnates • by Joanne Rock

Emma Layton desperately needs this job, but she's falling hard for her new boss, rancher Carson McNeill. And he might never forgive her when he finds out the secrets she's keeping about his family, and her connection to them all...

#2609 CRAVING HIS BEST FRIEND'S EX

The Wild Caruthers Bachelors • by Katherine Garbera

The one woman he wants is the one he can't have: his best friend's girlfriend. But when a newly single Chrissy goes to Ethan for comfort, things burn out of control. Until a test of loyalty threatens to end their forbidden romance before it begins...

#2610 FOBIDDEN LOVERS

Plunder Cove • by Kimberley Troutte

Julia Espinoza's true love was killed years ago...or so she believes. Until a stranger comes to town who looks and feels remarkably like the man she lost. Will this be the second chance she thought was lost forever? Or another of his parents' schemes?

———

Get 4 FREE REWARDS!

We'll send you 2 FREE Books plus 2 FREE Mystery Gifts.

Harlequin® Desire books feature heroes who have it all: wealth, status, incredible good looks... everything but the right woman.

FREE
Value Over
$20

SPECIAL EXCERPT FROM

HARLEQUIN® *Desire*

*Wealthy Texas politician Chase Ferguson ended things with his
ex to protect her. Yet now she's crashed his isolated vacation
house in a snowstorm. And when a stormbound seduction has
real-world repercussions, he must make a stand for what—and
who—he truly believes in.*

Read on for a sneak peek at
A Snowbound Scandal by Jessica Lemmon,
part of her **Dallas Billionaires Club** *series!*

Her mouth watered, not for the food, but for him.

Not why you came here, Miriam reminded herself sternly.

Yet here she stood. Chase had figured out—before she'd
admitted it to herself—that she'd come here not only to give
him a piece of her mind but also to give herself the comfort of
knowing he'd had a home-cooked meal on Thanksgiving.

She balled her fist as a flutter of desire took flight between her
thighs. She wanted to touch him. Maybe just once.

He pushed her wineglass closer to her. An offer.

An offer she wouldn't accept.

Couldn't accept.

She wasn't unlike Little Red Riding Hood, having run to the
wrong house for shelter. Only in this case, the Big Bad Wolf
wasn't dining on Red's beloved grandmother but Miriam's
family's home cooking.

An insistent niggling warned her that she could be next—and
hadn't this particular "wolf" already consumed her heart?

"So, I'm going to go."

When she grabbed her coat and stood, a warm hand grasped
her much cooler one. Chase's fingers stroked hers before lightly

squeezing, his eyes studying her for a long moment, his fork hovering over his unfinished dinner.

Finally, he said, "I'll see you out."

"That's not necessary."

He did as he pleased and stood, his hand on her lower back as he walked with her. Outside, the wind pushed against the front door, causing the wood to creak. She and Chase exchanged glances. Had she waited too long?

"For the record, I don't want you to leave."

What she'd have given to hear those words on that airfield ten years ago.

"I'll be all right."

"You can't know that." He frowned out of either concern or anger, she couldn't tell which.

"Stay." Chase's gray-green eyes were warm and inviting, his voice a time capsule back to not-so-innocent days. The request was siren-call sweet, but she'd not risk herself for it.

"No." She yanked open the front door, shocked when the howling wind shoved her back a few inches. Snow billowed in, swirling around her feet, and her now wet, cold fingers slipped from the knob.

Chase caught her, an arm looped around her back, and shoved the door closed with the flat of one palm. She hung there, suspended by the corded forearm at her back, clutching his shirt in one fist, and nearly drowned in his lake-colored eyes.

"I can stay for a while longer," she squeaked, the decision having been made for her.

His handsome face split into a brilliant smile.

Don't miss A Snowbound Scandal *by Jessica Lemmon, part of her* **Dallas Billionaires Club** *series!*

Available August 2018 wherever Harlequin® Desire books and ebooks are sold.

www.Harlequin.com

LOVE
Harlequin
romance?

Join our Harlequin community to share your thoughts and connect with other romance readers!

Be the first to find out about promotions, news, and exclusive content!

Sign up for the Harlequin e-newsletter and download a free book from any series at

www.TryHarlequin.com

CONNECT WITH US AT:

Harlequin.com/Community

 Facebook.com/HarlequinBooks

 Twitter.com/HarlequinBooks

 Instagram.com/HarlequinBooks

 Pinterest.com/HarlequinBooks

ReaderService.com

**ROMANCE WHEN
YOU NEED IT**

HSOCIAL2017